PRAISE FOR WATERFALL GIRLS

In Kimberly White's *Waterfall Girls*, you feel the mist of the rushing water against your skin. The writing is rich and deeply hypnotic, beckoning the reader to keep reading, and to fall. This is an absolutely beautiful and tragic book.

— CYNTHIA PELAYO, *INTO THE FOREST AND ALL THE WAY THROUGH*

A grotesque and lyrical trip into ecofeminism and collective story. *Waterfall Girls* conjure a neogothic precipice, the natural moments when death, mythos, and beauty dive into making the sublime.

— MONIQUE QUINTANA, AUTHOR OF *CENOTE CITY*

Kimberly White's *Waterfall Girls* oozes with lyrical beauty & wonder. At once experimental and reminiscent of ancient tragedies, I found myself captivated by every presence, every witness, every chorus of language. If you're looking for writing that will assist you in escaping wholly into a world of lore and originality, writing that will "force-[fill] your lungs and [wash] your consciousness through the veil", look no further than this stunning book.

— KAILEY TEDESCO, AUTHOR OF *FOREVERHAUS, LIZZIE, SPEAK, AND SHE USED TO BE ON A MILK CARTON*

In Kimberly White's new book *Waterfall Girls*, women climb, one by one, to the top of Waterfall to enact their suicides for many reasons. This remarkable poetic sequence is the river that ties them all together, in the voice of the Waterfall, attending nereids and fairies, and in the stories of the women themselves. It is both one long poem and a hundred separate poems, like sprays of water trickling back into a stream. Imagine an *anti-*Midsummer Night's Dream, a tragedy where the magic dust is administered too late, again and again. And yet we feel beauty and mystery in that missed connection: *"Waterfall speaks as an act of procession. Waterfall speaks as floating bridge; it does not choose the worlds it connects, and it speaks for neither."*

The reader's task is to dive into the deep current of this notebook of many voices. It's a long work, yes, but streams ever fresh – a book not *about* suicide but from *inside* it, as if each woman becomes part of the waterfall myth as she leaps, and her story is recast from different angles.

Come to this river of words and swim, and you will find more poetry in your life. You may need to come up for air, and then you will enter the water again. White's *Waterfall Girls* weaves a spell that the reader can inhabit: *"Where the light rises again, I sit on the shore, gaze into the waterfall for answers. There are none. There is scant revelation, only hypnotic voices and leaves of mystery."*

— BOB STANLEY, SACRAMENTO POET LAUREATE
EMERITUS, CO-DIRECTOR, UNIVERSITY
READING AND WRITING CENTER SACRAMENTO
STATE UNIVERSITY

WATERFALL GIRLS

KIMBERLY WHITE

CL◀SH

NEREID

I am Nereid, daughter of Amphitrite and Poseidon, who lives in the mist of the waterfall. I am what coats your skin and clings to your hair in tiny, heavy water beads. Those are my wet fingers streaking your face, and this is my warning to you: If you feel the urge to jump into this waterfall, first ask yourself, *where might it lead?*

Originally, I came from the sea, born before the first waterfall but destined to die in it.

Is it destiny when it's by your own hand, when it's your choice instead of the Gods'? Or does the fact that you made the choice and carried it out make it destiny? Here on the other side of the waterfall, the after-death side, *destiny* means *travesty* and by that I mean to say, *aspiration.*

As in *breath.* As a sea spirit, I adjusted to freshwater worlds by learning to breath a different air. An easy trick for a sea nymph who is also half-God. I moved easily back and forth from seawater to fresh, but sea was my natural habitat and the home to which I always returned. When I went into the waterfall, the jagged cliff rocks beat the sea water out of me while the churning maelstrom of fresh waterfall flushed both sea air and fresh air from my lungs, my gills and my veins. It is a very rough transition, and a very physical transformation.

When there is a suicide, everyone wants to know why.

There is one reason for suicide: escape. But there are more stories than can be articulated and counted, more than any one god or half-god can see. Why did I? Because the Mad God who made the waterfall also made me. Because I wanted not only to be excused from history, but to be exempt from it. Because I wanted to escape. Here on this side of the waterfall, I witness a different kind of history.

I have grown rich with witness.

Witness the first waterfall, when an Angry God threw a thunderbolt trident, split a mountain in two and created *Waterfall*.

Witness the first death in a waterfall: mine.

Some say a waterfall is a greedy thing that demands adoration and sacrifice. That with its first taste of blood, it became hungry.

After death, I no longer see the Waterfall as it was in my time and place on Earth. Here, it is impossible to see the Waterfall for all that it is. It changes with its own moods, with every new waterfall suicide it receives. Its appearance is shaped by the emotional states of the ones who jump, and by the appearance of the falls into which they jump. It could be that this Waterfall is every waterfall, and that every time a waterfall receives a suicide, I see yet another face of this Waterfall that is the genesis of every waterfall.

I am not the only thing that lives in this mist. Stories are told.

Every woman, every girl who commits suicide by waterfall comes here.

NEREID, DEFINED

He named me Nereid and because of it, I was one with the sea. He raised me to feel it, live it, breath it and because of it, I was one with the sea.

He exercised his Godly whims and because of it, I lost the sea. He made his waterfall, I jumped into it, driven by the misbelief of suicide. He tried to banish me from the sea and because of it, I banished him from me.

I have grown rich with witness. Everyone who jumps is jumping toward something. None here but Jenny have found it.

Some say that suicides never rest easy. Some claim the right to say who will rest and who won't, but there is no rest after death no matter what the cause; that is the real myth.

Yet rest is exactly what a suicide seeks.

This waterfall world is never still, even the elements are not static. Each new arrival brings her own questions, her own demons, adds her own subtle element, makes this world a little bigger, a little richer.

Is it the questions they bring with them which fuel the shifting shape of this world? My own questions are countless.

Warning: definitions shift their shapes here, too. *Weak* could mean *strong*, or *blue*, or *pear*. Or *weak*. *Strong* could mean *strong*, or *soothing*, or *pollen*. Once, *pollen* meant *bear*. This is the process by which elements shift. What I am compelled to witness cannot be defined in words that are guaranteed to mean the same thing when the ink is dry and their echo has faded.

Here, *defined* means *erased.*

I was the first to come here. Not the first *being* to come here, simply the first to come here by waterfall suicide. This world was already populated when I arrived. And I was received by very scrutinous eyes. Here, there is no subterfuge, no defenses, so it does not take long to be figured out by the creatures here who are not human, not nymph, not God. By whatever inscrutable criteria in place at the time, I was granted my place in this water Underworld.

Everyone who comes here also has their place, but few accept and embrace it. I do. Jenny does. Others too, so very few.

Before me, suicide was foreign to the Nereids, the sister spirits of the waters. And since I am here, I have no way to know if mine remains unique. Nereids are not so predictable as they are classically portrayed.

When I first came here, after I regained my definition and my senses, it was as if I was waiting for myself. I jumped into the waterfall because I no longer felt at home in my world, but here I am home. This does not make my choice right or wrong, it is a simple and straightforward consequence. Does that give me a sacred duty? Here, *sacred* means *floral, wisdomatic. Connective. Duty* has a much more nebulous feel - intertwined somehow, in a way that is more defiant than connective. I feel no urgency to untangle the ways in which this appears to me, here, now. Its own urgency will present itself at its own whim. I will be here to receive.

I have gone from harassing the Ishmaels of the ancient world to receiving the drowned and broken souls of suicide. We don't know what we really chose when we jump.

THE TASTE OF WATERFALL

Cold, why are waterfalls always cold? The first time it's tasted, by way of mist and spray on an outstretched tongue, the only thing there is *cold. Wet.* Step closer, the spray thickens but the taste is still... blank? clear?

But if you go down the falls, it is more likely they will taste of blood, teeth and bone. And then, the taste of drowning. The taste of water as it force-fills your lungs and washes your consciousness through the veil.

The taste of rock, your mortal grave as you dissolve in water, aided by fish and other nibblers, while you watch from the other side.

Best to taste it before you go in, however that comes to be.

SARAH THIRST

Sarah came from the desert, through a waterfall that is only there after a very heavy rain. Being of the desert, she knew this occasional waterfall. She has had two decades to study her desert, its rain, and its transitory waterfalls.

These desert girls are tough. Hardened by unremitting sun, heat, glare, their hard shells run deep. Despite the heat and dry earth of her native world, Sarah chose a water death, a rare event to frame the tragedy of her suicide. Here, on my side of the waterfall veil, she chafes against the amount of water that chains her to her own death, unfamiliar with the element of her eternity and unwilling to embrace it. There, her name was Sarah; here, her name is Thirst.

Thirst: the need to drink. A strong desire. To crave. A feeling of dryness in the mouth and throat. A material condition producing this desire. This, too is a material world.

Desert girls don't know how thirsty they really are. In the dryness of their environment, they are conditioned to keep their thirst in line with the innate scarcity of water, and this is a very hard thing to unlearn. This one, she craved things that drove her to the desert, to an even thirstier place, and she made the same mistake all suicides make: believing that cravings are escapable by death.

She is drawn by coyote voices both living and dead, into the desert that is her home. Not all that live in the desert are drawn to leave their comfortable neighborhoods to seek out the desert in the way Sarah did. Not all need to know the ghost towns with their little churches standing alone on hard ground, adobe martyrs rooted to stand even when their headstones have no more descendants. To know those narrow dirt roads so well she can drive them in her sleep, in her dreams of straight narrow lines cutting cloud swept basins of desert scrub, new worlds in sun, old worlds in shadow, invisible worlds in between.

Some temptations should only exist in dreams, the only concept surreal enough to hold such roads.

She seeks to read the script of the rippled dunes, each shifting grain precisely placed by the hand of the wind, by the bellies of snakes, and her own incongruous shoes, risking the poisons and dry-powder fire lurking in the intricate moving sands. She thirsts for the stark dryness, dry as if water had never been known, where water is remembered only in river-carved rocks more ancient than time. She feels the uprooted-ness: tumbling, blowing, falling, crumbling, scattered by wind and currents of forces faster than the eye and slower than the moon. She wonders if there were words for *stationary* in the ancient tongues of those who were drawn here before her.

In school, she takes up archeology as a way to connect with the desert, a way to know those who walked it before her. She digs, fingers old bones, re-assembles broken shards, sifts ancient dirt looking for lost dances which wind in the wind, spin the red dirt into whirlwinds, stamps the same dirt like the deer. She digs, deeper into the dirt, for a connection that eludes her. The more she digs, the less she understands the connection she craves. The more she thirsts.

In her dreams, the shadows of old worlds play their coyote tricks, and the temptations of invisible worlds raise their curious heads. They tease her, smell her vulnerability, taunt her with allusions to the magic of poison fangs, cactus flowers, promise the love of Fire Gods whose kisses burn hotter than the sun and promise the keys to ancient mysteries. Awake, she digs, looking for her desert but like the occasional waterfall that is there then slips away, the sacred connection promised in her dreams is absent in the displaced earth and rocks she runs through her fingers. The rotting fences strung beyond her ghost towns, with nothing left to hold, stand as monuments to her failure to contain that which will always be erased by the unseen, slowly consumed by insect and element. Unlockable mysteries, always out of reach.

The desire and delusion of suicide: the desire to escape and the delusion that they will be allowed to do so.

The church of archeology is not the answer. But she didn't know where to go from there - so much invested in something she ultimately could not use. So much poured into a false religion. It was to have been her *everything*.

Despite her disillusionment, she can't stay away from the desert. She is unable to escape its draw.

Escape. She never felt overtly suicidal, not even on her last day. Through her desert grapevine, she heard that the occasional waterfall was back and she went out alone, hoping to witness this rare spectacle in the peace of solitude. It was a strenuous hike, deep into the desert and up a serious cliff, the kind of hike one should never do alone. The weight of her spiritual and existential struggle had led to chronic insomnia and she was weeks without adequate sleep going into her solo hike to the waterfall. Most of it was familiar territory, vistas and plateaus that had always beckoned to her; but today it felt sinister, detached. Her worried mind, frayed and impaired from insomnia, became frantic - if she is not welcome here, in her beloved desert, if she cannot fit in even here, where? The work she did to get to know this desert, to connect with its mystery, overwhelms her now - how can she start again, do it all over again somewhere else, with something else? What if it's all for the same result, the same disappointment and disconnection?

By the time she reaches the top of the waterfall, the desert sun blazes high and her fatigue is crushing. She sits, closer to the edge than would someone with a better grip on their senses. She is stunned by the sight of so much water pouring down the cliff, the sensation of cool mist in the hot desert sun, drying as soon as it hits her burnt skin, and the roar, drowning out all conscious thought in her head. She is dizzy on top of that cliff and stands up to move away from the edge.

Instead, she hesitates, the toes of her boots peeking over the cliff edge. From her clifftop stance, she sees the sweeping vista of the desert in which she has lived and dug and searched. The desert which is her life. She casts out for the familiar draw of the desert, but instead, she feels the draw of the waterfall. She steps into a moment of fascination coupled with despair, and the waterfall brings her to me.

Long ago, I lost my curiosity for why they jump. I don't care why, but I see it anyway. Sometimes I see it as a geometric chart, lines of energetic influence bisect and converge from angles she never thought possible, a formula for a terrible end. Other times it is visual, as if her life is flashing before my eyes. The reasons are the same: craving, despair, escape. They will tell me anyway, some of them. Much of the time, it is on display when they jump. They think their feelings are unique to them, unable to see past their immediate pain, unable to envision a future without their pain but they are wrong, it is a very well-known and familiar pain.

Desert waterfalls, brief fleeting streams that come and go with thunderstorms and flash floods; they come with power. They come with voice. Water in the desert is a mercurial thing, yet the desert is shaped by water. Water and wind carved the ways for flash flood streams; wind is ever-present but water is almost a rare event. To die by desert waterfall is even more rare and generally can't be planned. If it happens, it is one who is already on that edge, who has a chance encounter with one of those transient flows and is overcome, who takes a spontaneous step of faith.

But transient waterfalls are no different than any other waterfall, on my side of the veil. The length of their earthly existence is immaterial when all waterfalls are one. Here, the Waterfall lurches and heaves, becomes that fleeting desert waterfall and the portal is open for Sarah poised on a sharp crag, ready to join the insistent flood streaming down dry desert cliff.

Like many in that moment, she pauses for a split second, deliberately takes her last breath and holds it. A deep breath, as if the amount of air in her lungs will matter. The memory of my own last breath takes hold and I hold mine as she dies, as she's battered to the bottom by the churning falls.

Later, when she has collected herself and can sit coherently on my shore, she is aware but confused. They are always confused. This is not what they expect to see, this is not where they expect to be. The waterfall still looks like hers; like a womb that has just given birth, it has not yet regained its customary shape and she has not yet grasped the difference.

She has not yet grasped that she is still thirsty for what she craved; that realization will be longer in coming. She has not yet grasped that she really is dead, that it is irrevocable.

All that she has not yet grasped cannot be listed, because even I do not grasp it all.

THIRST STORIES

She wanders here, Sarah Thirst, still in search of her lost desert world. She thirsts here as she did there, dry and starved in this too-wet world. Whatever she thought would be waiting for her on the other side of her waterfall, she expected it to match her known world. There is comfort in the familiar, despite the suicidal need for a different world. So much water, so much green here; she is a dry creature in a wet land. She shivers, missing her desert heat, but it is warm enough here. Her demons take delight in tricking her into the water, shoving her head underwater to remind her that she breathes just as well in wet as in dry.

Still, she clings to her discomfort. When the eels come onto the land, she mistakes them for rattlesnakes, confused by their wings. The constant sound of the waterfall, no matter how far she thinks she wanders, is repulsive to her, like the sound of earth disgorging something noxious. Yet it is she who holds her ears out of tune with this world. She craves the feel of the sun burning her skin, but there is no sun here, nothing burns. Our sky is lit by a different source.

She craves that which she sought by suicide: the granting of what her life lacked. Her death was not something she longed and planned for over time, it was a fatal impulse sparked by longtime disillusionment and the sudden encounter with the waterfall. An impulse which would have been just a symptom, had she not been standing on the cliff edge of the waterfall when it hit. Growing up in her desert city, she had been led to believe that hers would be an easy road, but it wasn't always that way. There were failed romances, the unmasking of familial hypocrisy, abandonment by ones she thought were lifelong friends. There were hard and necessary adjustments, which she was still making when she died. Putting all of her hopes for answers into her studies, and the heartbreak of disappointment when she realized it wasn't going to fill the gaping holes in her spirit.

On a humid desert day after a gut-busting thunderstorm, there is water everywhere. On the minimal, slippery track she follows up a steep cliff to the spectacular and seldom-seen waterfall, she does not have death on her mind. There is a palpable sense of danger as she ascends. Awed by the radiance of the soaking-wet desert, she is afraid of it at the same time. Her sense of disconnection is amplified by all of this water, an unexpected interloper coming between her and her desert.

Desert girl that she is, she has seen wet desert before. She has seen plenty of waterfalls. Water in the desert always feels foreign but today, it feels almost hostile. She thinks about slipping, falling in, going down and not coming back up, with a dispassion that is comforting in her state of mind.

Until she reaches the top of the waterfall, and her world-view is spread out before her. The crashing sound of the waterfall drowns out the clatter of her worried mind and she feels all that she ever believed herself to be, erased by the sound, washed away with the falls. The empty space that was left could only be filled by the water.

She made sure her camera caught the sight of the waterfall, virgin before she went in. Those she left behind found the things she left at the edge of the waterfall, now gone, dried up almost as soon as she put it on the map. Her camera contained images of a sight never before recorded in that part of the desert: a waterfall previously known only by rumor and unverified sightings. Opportunity is a fluid thing - the opportunity to escape is always in the mind of a prisoner and not all stop to think about where they might be escaping *to*. Not all stop to think about what is on the other side of that leap.

In her desert town, the most interesting thing to do was to get to know the desert around her. She learned the rocks and trails, flora and fauna, the tricks to surviving the harsh, inflexible desert. She hiked known and unknown trails, relied on the dry desert dust to preserve her footprints and mark the road home. Here, the green grass springs back to its original shape as soon as her foot moves to the next step and she loses herself in an unmarkable place. She is confused by the unfamiliarity of the verdant velvet cushion of this world, why her afterlife doesn't resemble the sharp earthen edges of the world she left behind. Like everyone here, she wants things to make sense, but she cannot move beyond the dry brown perimeters of what she tried to bring with her when she jumped. In the loose, inchoate assumptions of her unconscious mind, she thought she would stay in the desert after her death, become one with her beloved desert, a holy desert ghost who would join the legends still whispered in native tongues and enhanced by popularity and subculture. One who could lay claim to this desert as her own, by virtue of dying in it.

But virtue is not what she believed it to be and here, the permanence of her impulsive suicide weighs more heavily upon her than the demons who followed her down. In her wandering rejection of this world, she is eager to erase the mistake of her suicide. She approaches the waterfall as something to be overcome, tries to escape this oppressive, damp green by climbing back up the waterfall by which she came. But the waterfall will slap her down, again and again, ruthless in its boundary and relentless in its insistence that this is her world now, this is the consequence she could not anticipate when she jumped, she cannot kill herself twice in the same waterfall.

Thirst is a multi-layered craving of justification and need, and here, necessity is tempered with both blindness and trust. Here, *trust* does not equate *faith*, and faith is not a word that is translatable here. We all learn it the hard way.

THE WATERFALL SPEAKS

H ere, elemental becomes diselemental. What does that have to do with Water? But Waterfall is more than just water, and it can be said that Waterfall is an act, not an element. Here, the act is the same, whatever the element.

Some say the voice of Waterfall speaks as element rather than mass, but the truth is, Waterfall speaks as an act of procession. Waterfall speaks as floating bridge; it does not choose the worlds it connects, and it speaks for neither.

Waterfall was born when Poseidon heaved his trident into a seashore cliff and split it open, causing Waterfall to spill forth in a primal gush of long-awaited release. A floating bridge was born, a connection between worlds, a place where one world crashes into another.

Waterfall was not created to be a weapon. Whatever the intentions of the Mad God who made me, my own form and intent is shaped by me, not him. These are the same words Nereid used to fling at him, the same God who made her. So what makes Waterfall such a tempting vehicle for suicide? Vehicle, as a soft way of saying **weapon**. Legends grow among the people left behind as a way to explain, even heroify the unspeakable. They accuse the Waterfall of being greedy, create stories and sacrificial traditions of the greedy Waterfall, must feed the waterfall.

But Waterfall has no hunger, it cannot be **fed** in the known

*meaning of that word. On Nereid's side of the waterfall, **to feed**
means **to blossom**, and a waterfall is already in full bloom.*

Greedy waterfall, feed the falls. *Ones who die this way, by being
thrown into a waterfall to satisfy a social demand for sacrifice, are
not committing suicide. The do not come to rest in Nereid's world.*

*It is the nature of Waterfall to carry, to carve and break down.
This is the definition of a tool, not a weapon. Waterfall serves this
purpose as the hand of Creator Gods, shaping element with element.
Later hands have even harnessed the waterfall for electricity, power
for power, but a manmade waterfall is still a waterfall. It might not
possess the same natural beauty, but the power is much the same. Just
as some Ancients enslaved themselves to waterfalls, so today do some
enslave themselves to the dam, the power plant. All in service to the
power of the waterfall. Sacrifices will always be made. Unlike the
Ancients, they are rarely made directly by throwing someone into the
manmade falls; they are more private, subtle. But sacrifice by any
subtlety is still a price that someone believes must be paid.*

*Such as it is with suicide. One who commits suicide does so with
the belief that their life is a necessary price to pay for something -
escape, redemption, release. Only after the irrevocable act do they
learn that the Universe does not barter in lives. Some would label me
sacred, including Nereid, but we know what that really means.
Unpredictable power should be approached with caution, but
untouchable goes too far.*

*Under such a changing face, my bones also crack and erode. The
waterfall you see today will be a little farther upriver the next time
you come. My jagged lip will be smoother here, sharper there, and a
breakaway rivulet will become my main cataract. Even on Nereid's
side of the waterfall, this is true. It simply happens at a different pace.*

*Some wonder: something such as a waterfall born in a fit of
immortal rage, how can it not embody that anger? Witness the size,
the fearsomeness, the appetite of some waterfalls.*

*Witness also the small waterfalls, even the miniatures. How they
emanate beauty, enchantment; how they invite you to swim without
danger, how they embrace you when you stand under their shallow
surge. Greed and bloodthirstiness are not what you feel. The destructive power of erosion of even the tiniest waterfall is not what you feel.
Life is what you feel. Alive and connected to something rare, mystical.*

Can a waterfall step outside of itself, study and observe itself as humans purportedly do? Perhaps. But why? Waterfall does not possess intent, craving. It does one thing: it falls. Magnificence and spirit are in the eye of the observer. My voice, like any, can be manipulated. Manufactured. Voices in heads, prayers, books, from above, below and within might be real, might be manufactured, might be manipulated. Enhanced by the favored flavors of the ones who hear them.

Like voice, there is no beauty that cannot be subjected to enhancement. It's the impatient human drive for more, better. Natural process is not enough. The Ancients made their sacrifices to get more from the Waterfall, to get more from life. Suicides make their sacrifice to be granted exemption from natural process.

But the process doesn't stop with the dive. Downriver, through the rapids, the river digests, breaks down and excretes. They are not what they once were. It is a first step in learning that nothing remains the same, not even after death, no matter how slow the change, and suicide does not speed up the process.

When the Waterfall splits itself into smaller waterfalls within the waterfall, it shows multiple sides of the same face. When the Waterfall fragments into trillions of droplets of mist, some never landing on anything solid, it reaches out beyond its form, touches that which comes close enough to judge. When other things manifest in the mist, the Waterfall reveals itself as more than a singular world.

OPENING

I love to watch the Waterfall change.

It starts like deep breathing, a swelling and contracting of form, waterfall muscles heave and quiver and things get a little blurry. The gyrations are different each time, both in length and rite. A shapeshift takes place. It is still Waterfall, but now, it is a different waterfall.

There is a distinct preparation process for each one who comes through. I am not privy to all of it, except to know that it runs far deeper than even I, half-God and half-nymph, can begin to know. It takes its own time, and we know what *time* means here. Shorter, longer, variations of both, always different. Length of time matters not to me - for all I know, I am here for eternity, so the deeper my view of this process, the more interesting is my world.

The Waterfall gyrates: have you ever seen a waterfall stretch? Picture yoga, but a waterfall. It's very confusing to observe, because I am swept in and disoriented – it's almost like going over the falls again, but in a slow velvety way, without the brutal battering of the first time. In a way, sexual - the painful and awkward loss of virginity versus the slip-slide grace of mature sex.

And then someone new comes through. Most times, I am witness to what leads to her leap into the falls and the battering which brings her here. I don't know if she sees me watching, but it doesn't matter. Witness has its privilege.

It's all about her last day. The last day of her life, before she jumps. Often, the events and emotions of her life leading up to this suicide edge are what overtakes her mind and her reasoning, memories and feelings relived with the raw burning of years. I see all of that as well. And then she is here, heaving and bewildered on the shore. I leave her to herself, until she finds her own place here.

Some never do. Rather, some have not yet, despite being here for hundreds, thousands of countable years.

While she recovers herself, I am still fixated, mesmerized by the waterfall. It takes a while for it to regain its customary appearance, however that is defined. Sometimes it stays that way, as a recognizable place on a postcard, until it changes again for the next one to come through.

As such, I am rich with witness.

The transition from the portal opened by the newest one, back to the sight and motion of the Waterfall as I know it, the Waterfall of all waterfalls, is a process all its own. Once again, I have all the time that can be imagined to bear witness. The fluid yogic twists unfold almost in reverse, but in a sideways manner until it regains the shape with which I am most familiar.

Here, *sideways* means *fractal, geometric, concentric*. It's even harder to translate into waterfall words. To translate from waterfall words.

THE HONEYMOON BRIDE

Sometimes they find me. They wring themselves out and see me, sitting peacefully watching them and those who do not run from me on sight, come to me. They have questions. They don't know what happened, where they are. Some fight what I tell them, angry that I don't have satisfactory answers, angry that they are not where they hoped they would be. Angry that they will have to keep searching for their God. This one is hungry, so she says. Here, *hungry* means *hungry* but it also means *fresh*. Only the new ones are hungry. She asks me for food, but I suppose she can eat anything she sees and see what happens.

She is angry and puzzled by my response, then reaches for a fern. The fern pulls out of her grasp and hisses like a snake, adding to her confusion. She turns to walk away, plucks a leaf from a low-hanging branch but now, she has no mouth. She wanders off, drops the useless leaf, which climbs, inchworm-like, slowly up the trunk and back to the branch from which it was plucked.

Here, the trees and plants and green growing things behave much like they do in most other worlds, unless they are disturbed. Here, they do not serve as food, shelter or resources. Here, they are autonomous.

Of course, there are disturbances. This is a world of broken spirits.

I've seen this one before. Her hunger is powerful, but she has been here for so long she no longer remembers what she is hungry for. She should have gotten over her hunger as bodily desire long ago, but her kind of hunger is also her demon. She came through the Waterfall as a honeymoon bride, or what passes for honeymoon in her place and time. What drives a newlywed to suicide on her honeymoon?

Disappointment.

Humiliation.

Rage.

This one had no room for rage; in her time and place, rage was the privilege of men. A woman's place allowed no rage. Her disappointment and humiliation gave no room. A potent cocktail when there is a weapon at hand, and the waterfall was her weapon. Hungry all of her life, but not for food, and her hunger dominates her death.

This honeymoon bride, who was hungry all of her life but not for food, she had her own distorted picture of beauty and her bridal ideal. Anorexia in a wedding dress. But when the dress came off and she was only bones, her new husband, a man with far more money than sympathy, was outraged. She was only bones. There was no flesh and blood bride to bed, only bones. He was cruel. *Disgusting bones.* How could a woman like her, with *breeding* and *means* be starved? What kind of lunatic? Crazed, he accused her and her family of conspiring to defraud him of the full value of his entitlement as a husband. He called her every ugly name he could imagine, then threw her out, for the dog to bury, he said. She threw herself into the waterfall.

When she came here, she brought her skeleton and her wedding dress. I can still see the bones under the layers of silk and lace. She tells me she is hungry, and walks away unsatisfied.

As for the chatter that lived on after her, the loudest came from her well-monied husband. How could she starve in the lap of luxury? What kind of people? How could they *let* her? In her day, they didn't have a name for it. It was very rare and very, very secret. No one saw anything wrong before she was undressed on her wedding night and the story of her self-starvation was baffling to all. The fact of her sudden suicide was lost in the bewilderment of anorexia. Insanity was the only label they could choose, and in her time, wasn't suicide the sanest act an insane person could undertake? The grief of her loss and the resulting chatter had much more to do with position and politics than it did with love.

THE SCENT OF WATERFALL

E lectric, but without the dry static on which electricity rides. How to describe the scent of wet, of drowning? How it's sharp in your nostrils as your olfactory glands grasp for something to identify but instead, they are paralyzed by the sudden wet charge. How it eradicates all other scents. The air is coated, soaked with wet and the power present in each molecule penetrates all senses.

Some will say that fresh water has no scent. Chlorine, salt, sewage, they will describe the scent of water by what pollutes it. But in the absence of additives, they will say there is no scent. Some will say that water bears the scent of everything it erodes and collects along the way; the scent of all sediment.

But falling water is more than just water. Now, falling, ionization is involved. Particles are transformed and reborn as something...else. The antennae of your nose hairs will recognize the subtle radiation process of ionization, by which molecules collide and react and turn each other into other things...the antennae of your nose hairs will catch the electricity passing through...your conscious mind will not recognize such things but the antennae of your nose hairs are connected to more channels than just your conscious mind.

Breathe in deep. Feel how the waterfall makes you feel the danger of drowning, even when only close enough to smell it.

Breathe out, remember you are not underwater. You will still taste it.

Drowning in it changes the smell, as your physical death adds its own scent. Drowning fills more than just your lungs with water. All senses as you know them are washed away. Upon your death, your own scent is added to the scent of all sediment, to overflow with the falls and paralyze in turn the senses of the ones who stand behind on the shore.

DEMONS

I see the demons who follow them. Not in the corporeal way - here, *corporeal* means more than the sum of elements or senses. They see them too, flickering in and out of sight, swat at them like flies.

Most are about the size of gnats. They have no need for bulk here, they need only exist and be present. It could be said that this is a demons' playground, where they have shapeshift power and delight in disguising themselves as eels, faces in the rocks, butterflies, and even as Jenny. They conspire among themselves, even trade places sometimes, but they never lose sight of their real targets.

Only Jenny has no demons of her own, so maybe she really is one of them. Or all of them. I can't even be sure that she doesn't see them - if she does, she keeps it close, but there are little hints. I am the suspicious type.

Don't think of a demon as being something necessarily evil, although they can be that. These are not that kind of demon. These demons are reminders, tiny fierce embodiments of what follows you from there to here, the things that will not be escaped by committing suicide.

It's not clear if the others understand that. They swat them away, curse at them, ignore them in turn, but still their tiny flying demons persist. Some things will not be swatted away, or washed away by a waterfall.

A demon is simply a reminder. Not an evil thing, not a benevolent thing, a reminder. Small and big as they can be, their eyes are piercing, they trail unnatural lights and some have friends. They have voices, but I do not hear them. I see them taunt, I see them laugh, but I do not hear. I see their games, which are not games, but remembrances, nettlesome memories of failures, humiliations, rejections and other things that haunt bothered minds; capsules of hatred, disgust, mortification, re-enacted as games. I see them pose as leaves, lady-bugs, rocks, fish, and other beings unimaginable *there*. A dandelion puffs out and blows in the moist breeze, the floating bits of down are thousands of even tinier demons, all belonging to one waterfall-bound soul.

Some are mirrors, wearing mocking faces that stare back distorted with pathos, bathos, abysmal echoes of all that led to the waterfall. All are tricksters. They are as much a part of this place as the Waterfall itself.

LOST

This one's name is lost to history. She had a name, but it was sacrificed for family and for the era. Here, her name is Lost, because here, that is the only word she has ever said.

She came from a time and place where women were inconsequential, but for the children they could bear. Their lives were traded and discarded like leftover bones and they had nothing with which to bargain on their own behalf; even their fecundity was considered male property. An unfortunate time and place, for a woman, where there was no notion of other times, places, or mindsets and no other roles for her. In so many respects, the more you know, the more you crave, and certain forms of knowledge are bound to seep through whatever limitations humans believe they can set. Such were the things for which a woman could be executed in her world.

So when her children came, her purpose was fulfilled, and any kind of craving she felt was channeled into love for her children. But she lost her children to the waterfall, two promising and valued boys, and a girl, the child of her heart. It was a tragic accident and she was left with nothing but the magnitude of her devastation. Because without them, she was nothing.

Shunned for her loss, even though she wasn't at fault, and

with few choices, she returned to the waterfall that broke her heart and followed them in, but accidents and suicides don't go to the same place. When she emerged from her transitional stupor, she said one thing: *Lost.*

Before I could answer her (*we are all lost*), she moved on to the next one she could see. *Lost,* she said. *Lost,* she said to everyone she could see. To the younger ones, it was a question: *Lost?*

When she found Jenny, she was overcome. *Lost,* she cried, trying to wrap Jenny in a mother's hug. But Jenny is not lost. And Jenny has not learned sympathy; she flew away and Lost does not see her anymore. Whether she won't or can't, I don't know.

There was very little chatter when she died. Her erasure was decreed by her time and her loss was suppressed at the deepest levels. She will not find her children here. Having never fully opened there, she will not open up here. She has only one story: *lost,* the only word she has ever said here. I imagine she did not say much more *there,* limited not by ability, but by society to words like *food, offering, please.* Basic needs. *Pregnant.* Basic purpose. Here, *lost* means *transitory,* or it did until she came.

Here, she does nothing but wander. Once in a while, I see her with Celestine, joining forces in search of their lost children. They join up and split apart again, wander the waters and the lands and test the boundaries in their fruitless searches. They do not believe me when I tell them their children are not here. Once, after I said so, Celestine attacked me, pinned me down and strangled me with vicious, angry hands until it finally became clear to her that she could not kill me. She tried to spit in my face before letting me go, but that also failed because here, we do not pay for each others' sins.

We are all lost here. No one yet has come here who is named Found.

THE BOATMAN

S ome might be shocked to know of my affair with the Boatman. He is known by other names in other traditions, all of which are simply much more ancient words for Boatman. Once, I asked him which name he preferred, and he shrugged. They are all his names, but none truly *name* him.

We have known each other a very long time, the Boatman and I. He is the one thing that can move between the worlds and he was ancient before I was born, before my father was born, but he has become much younger since my death.

Being the watery thing I have always been, I encountered him often in my formative years. Always shadowy, always silent. Intense, fire eyes of obsidian, those black eyes see all, know all, communicate far more than the capability of words.

When I was young, I would see him plying in the secluded waterways, always alone, his boat empty. This was - and is - not the same ferry boat ridden by the souls of the dead to the mouths of their underworlds. This is his personal boat. I and the other water beings stayed away from his ferry crossings; the water there is unhealthy. Inhospitable, polluted as they are by the souls who refuse to accept their death, who jump in the water to escape the Boatman and where they rot, imprisoned by the river, until they relent and accept their fate. But away from those places, in his small private boat, he is most hospitable.

When I went into the waterfall, I expected to wake up in his ferry boat. I was very surprised to emerge here, on this side of the waterfall, without his stewardship. It was not until some-time later, after the disorientation had faded, that I saw him here, watching me from his small boat in the shadows. Imme-diately, I felt protected and at home. He kept his distance for quite a while, but eventually came closer and soon, it was as if old friends had never parted.

There, he never speaks verbally. Here, he speaks eloquently. But he never speaks of the other world, the world I left behind. That is a silence he does not break. But no matter. We find plenty to talk about in this world and far beyond. He is a man of cosmic mystery, filling an epic role that the Gods themselves do not have the stomach to take on. He unwinds however he can and sometimes, it is with me.

Some of the others see him, not many. The ones who do say little, and try not to show themselves. He observes them all, and provides interesting insight when he pleases. I will prob-ably spend eternity trying to figure out this world and its other inhabitants, so I listen to what he offers. I cannot know if it's true. I also do not know what good it would do me to know what is true here, where *true* means *fluid*, because this is a well-watered world.

Would any fluid world be complete without a Boatman?

He takes me for rides, softly plies the hidden ways of this world. Silent, his boat glides without effort. With a wave of his hand, passages open and close behind us, sealed by thick bushy branches, sly boulders or a trick of mist. It is a loud quiet on these deserted waters: the deep course of the stream, dark undercurrents adding their own voice, the whispered stares of the cliff faces that blanket us in, the dip of his oar as we pass.

We pass graffiti, ancient marks engraved on the cliff face by anonymous hands, unreadable to me. I know he reads them, perhaps he writes them. He smiles as we pass, as if they tell familiar and beloved tales. They will not be revealed to me. The passage curves, narrows, widens again and the trees change, subtle, less leafy in the familiar sense of the word. Now they are feathery, tendrilled, birdwinged. There is sky but it is not *sky*, it does not accommodate high flight, so the bird-trees remain rooted.

I am skeptical of these witnesses, but he assures me they have no eyes. No, but they smell, they hear. But, he says, they do not know how to *witness* in ways that concern me.

He glides the small boat to an inlet where the trees are more like stones, where the grass grows with blades thick and round like fat yarn fingers. Here, where there is no hint of witness, the thick green grass makes a welcome bed. On days like this, there is no gray in his beard, no wrinkle on his skin, which is not *skin* in the human sense of the word, as he is far older than human. Far younger than Divine. But skin that is not skin arouses, responds, radiates between us, envelops us in the fusion of more than mere body parts. The velvet green beneath us softens and bends to our form, matches our rhythm in quakes and shudders.

Because here, time is not time, he can linger until we are both spent - not in the physical sense of the word, but in a way that both mirrors and transcends physical. After, we talk about what it means to bear witness, how the pain of it and the joy of it can be indistinguishable. We talk about mythology, the logic and hope of it and the absurdist despair of it. We talk about prophecy, how it creates and destroys itself and its followers. We talk about innocence, debate whether it is enhanced or washed away by the Waterfall.

He takes a different route back to where he picked me up, another passage unknown to me. Just before he kisses me goodbye until next time, he whispers a secret. A riddle: the Waterfall has a sister. Sisters. Many sisters.

Many sisters
By way of a waterfall:
where ancient victims go
where sacrificial victims go
where murder victims go
where men go

BOATMAN STORIES

He is one with his vessel. He wears a face carved by the rivers connecting all worlds, unerasable by transmigration and unscarred by time, recognized by all as his own. On the days when he elects to be mine, he finds me waiting on the shore, ripe and ready for my turn to be the center of his attention.

When there is nobody waiting at his docks, he comes to me. He brings the fares he has extracted, mere moments of memories of exquisite life, tucked safely away until we are curled up in a secret cove. There, they are sipped like wine, in those private moments of night that are not night, not day.

Most souls cross his river but once, but I have crossed it with him again and again. When sentenced for my sins by Poseidon, I rode the last journeys of the victims of my reckless follies, held their hands in penance, endured their angry curses. After they reached their afterlife shore, it was just me and the Boatman on the peaceful return, often by a longer and more scenic way than the dark crossings of my drowned sailors. Sometimes, he would share a minor secret or story about one of the sailors who had been particularly savage in his assessment of me, to soften my guilt just a little bit.

He likes the trickster in me.

And he is not in league with Poseidon.

Despite my confinement here, he ferries me. Places open and concealed, stretching the boundaries of this world as they confine me, the familiar recast through my waterfall eyes, the unfamiliar open to me again. Through him, I hear, I see the ones left behind by the others, devastated by suicide, their questions and laments fighting to pierce the boundaries of their world. From my vantage point, their cries take on forms similar to the demons attached to their loved ones on this side of the Waterfall, similar to my own demons. I wonder what would happen if the barriers were penetrated. They so desperately want to hear each other, reach each other, but all I can do is watch. Listen.

He who opens these doors holds the key to lock them tight away, and his boat goes only where he wants it to go. He is adept at living half in dark, one eye hooded and always accustomed to dim light, one eye revealed with double catchlights in perfect sync. Flawless sight in both worlds.

His smile is rarely revealed in the light, rarer in the dark. But I know it well.

ANOESIS, ACCORD

S tep into a moment of blue, white-blue churning mass a roar that drowns out all possible thought. Count the voices in that roar, if you can. A state of pure waterfall, nothing else.

Some hear these voices and think they hear community. Some confuse community with accord. There is no accord in suicide. There is plurality, but little community on this side of the Waterfall. Small societies form and mutate and dissolve, but we are not One.

Suicide is an act of displacement, an unreconciled canvas, like a sea nymph trapped in a waterfall. Displaced by my own hand, I am bound by the boundaries of my act. Every suicide leads to a different end, regardless of the weapon. Pick your suicide, pick your hell. Picking a waterfall leads to the backside of all waterfalls.

Even without the earthly memories, we here are still who we were before the Waterfall. Ourselves, yes, but less. Much is washed out by the massive meatgrinder of the falls, which acts as filter to ensure that which belongs on that side stays on that side.

When they arrive, they are themselves, but not. They will feel incomplete when they finally come around, and that takes time. And that does not include the ones who have yet to awaken here after their waterfall ride, the ones who lay restless, sleeping where I have dragged them off to the side, under a rocky canopy where they are lined up in neat rows. Waiting to awaken.

Here, time is not so inflexible. Just a few days ago, two of the sleeping beauties woke up, one who has been here for almost as long as I, the other a much shorter time. It's not an instantaneous awakening – they are often quite disoriented when they come to. At first, they simply feel sensations, emotions, pure states uncontained by cognitive thought; a state that is both peaceful and disturbed. Suicide never brings real peace, and the disturbed part of this state is the unrealized beginning of that eternal weight.

Slowly, the self is re-formed, the parts of self that make it through the falls. The process becomes more fraught with the remembrance of themselves, and the slow and painful recognition that suicide did not solve their problems. Their demons came right along with them.

I have grown rich with witness. They struggle to forget while wearing their histories in their eyes. I read their stories, not just in their eyes, but in the Waterfall, the rocks, the grass, trees, the poems that compose themselves and attach like demons. It is all readable to me.

Sometimes, they find me. They stumble and wander in and out of my sight, appear, disappear, one or more at the same time. They want answers and I have none. I have only been here longer. I want answers from them: Why do you ask me? I show them with my eyes that I am dead like them. Is not my own history written in my eyes, in this land, like theirs, can they not read like I do? I too want answers from the Universe: why? where? how? how long? Nothing is fixed in the Universe. Ever.

They stepped into a moment of *nothingness*, where they sought sweet release, but true release is not found in this watery world. Here, *nothing* means *cloaked, secret*. They complain of being trapped in the very waterfall that killed them, but the waterfall did not kill them. It was merely the gun in their hand.

OTHER BRIDES

There are other Brides here. Women have been escaping their marriages by suicide for quite some time, and some go by waterfall.

Some came on their honeymoon. The weight of expectations can be astronomical and disappointment, immense. Waterfalls, being popular honeymoon spots, are already there. Some are Anniversary Brides. They come back to the waterfall for different reasons, some accompanied, some alone, bloated with disgust for their marriage. They see the analogy of the battering force of the falls, feel the weight of their lives driving them down to a rocky bottom from which they can't escape.

Suzette, an Anniversary Bride, comes alone back to the falls where she first honeymooned. It was such an uncertain time, her honeymoon so long ago, that she questions whether any of it really happened. The patina of time wears all things thin.

Don't all marriages start with uncertainty? The definitions and purposes of marriage have evolved in so many different directions over eons, but uncertainty is an unwavering thread. Way back then, Suzette had no idea what she faced. What she accepted when she said *I do*. And now, so many years gone, she is back to the place that is the symbol of the beginning of her end. Her honeymoon waterfall.

On her last day, she woke up hungry, and ate a breakfast at the lodge that could have fed three large people. Ravenous, she cared not about her weight, her cholesterol, or the size of the check, she just ate. It was the best meal of her life, the only peaceful and uninterrupted meal she had had since her marriage. With that, she felt the best way to honor the blessedness of such a meal was to never eat anything again. In other words, to die with this happy belly.

And the waterfall... such splendor, such majesty. Such symbolic power over the hopes and dreams of so many who come here to honeymoon in its mist. When she left her home last night, while her odious husband snored in front of the TV, she left an anniversary card on the nightstand. She crossed out all the tender sentiments in the card and substituted words of contempt, then signed it, *Fuck You.*

Words she had never, could never say to him any other way, for fear of violence.

Today, she gives herself the anniversary gift she most wants: solitude. Over breakfast, reveling in her splendid isolation, she reviews the anniversary gifts he has given her over the years:

A hunting rifle for him to borrow. It was his favorite joke every hunting season - *Hey Honey, you don't mind if I borrow your anniversary rifle, do ya? Ha!*

A lawnmower. He never mowed the lawn again. *It's your lawnmower, Babe. That makes it your job, HA! Happy Anniversary!*

Barbeque tools, with which she was required to barbeque for him and his bull-snorting friends for every televised sporting event that caught his fancy. Refusal bought a black eye.

Outrageous lingerie. Refusal to put it on bought her a broken tooth. Once on, he ridiculed her body, told her she was dressed like the worthless slut that she was, shoved her to the floor and raped her. A separated shoulder to go with her bloody tooth.

Leaving him didn't help. He tracked her down, broke her down, dragged her back down. She hated her anniversary worse than any other day of the year, more than his birthday.

So, that was the day she picked to go, to say it all in her special altered anniversary card and *go*.

Now, at the falls where it all began, she tries to remember why she said *I do*. She was young, fragile, and he was charming, forceful. She didn't know there were such things as warning signs. On their honeymoon, they stood together on this very spot, at the top of the roaring waters and he told her to take a good look at this waterfall and remember it, because if she ever did him wrong in any way, he would drag her back here and throw her in. It was the first time she heard him use that voice, colder and harder than ice. From then on, every time he spoke to her, no matter how tender or charismatic he was trying to be, she still heard that voice simmering underneath, straining its leash.

It's a slow day in the chilly off-season, and she is nearly alone at her vantage point. One or two couples, fewer singles, come to *ooh* and *ahh* and take a few pictures, then off they go to the next waterfall sight. None see her. Clouds move in overhead, bring an odd hush to overlay the roar of the falls and she feels peace, freedom, light. Calm, she waits for one last couple to leave and then she is alone. She climbs the rail and hesitates, holds her breath, then laughs at herself for doing so. Exhale, another deep breath, and she jumps.

The battering is brief before she is dead, before she hits the bottom.

There are the Unwilling Brides. Brides forced into marriage, for whom there is no concept of happiness and certainly no honeymoon. Self-destruction, in their times, is easy, and they take it. But they are dissatisfied in this place, longing for something but not knowing *what*. There wasn't enough for them in their time and place to find who they really are.

In Rohini's world, there was no concept of choice in marriage. There are few choices of any kind for women in her world. Her marriage was arranged before she could walk and carried out before she began to bleed. She was enslaved, brutalized by her husband's family. Her husband was not much older than her and like her, knew only what his family taught him. Tribal customs are deeply entrenched and they are not questioned. She was burdened with all of the family dirty work, being too young to prove herself as a mother.

Every day, she was checked for blood. For reasons she didn't understand she was stripped naked by the elder females of the family and rudely examined for signs of menarche. On the day they found it, she was thrown in a dark shed and locked away for seven days. On the day she was freed, she was given a ritual bath and locked up again, this time in a chamber with her husband, who had been instructed on how to rape her.

And rape her he did. Every night. During the day, she was slave to the family, at night she was slave to his rapes. When her blood came again, she was beaten by her teenaged husband, then by the women of his family, for not being pregnant. When her cycle ended, the rapes began again. When she still failed to become pregnant, she was beaten again. There was not a day when her slight body was not consumed with pain. Her workload was increased and the beatings became more fierce. She became pregnant and the beatings stopped; she miscarried and was beaten nearly to death. She became pregnant again and delivered a daughter.

Her baby girl wasn't wanted by her husband and his family. The baby was thrown into the local waterfall as an offering to the Fertility God, with fervent prayers for a boy child, for an army of boy children.

She was left alone with her grief, a grief she didn't know was possible. It was certainly not acceptable. The grief and depression were paralyzing and after a while, they stopped trying to beat her out of it and she was left alone in a shed with the goats. They didn't even bother to lock it. If she ate, she ate what the goats ate.

After a few weeks, she crawled out, waiting until late at night when the family would be asleep. Careful not to disturb the goats and awaken anyone, she crept slowly through the compound and out to the road. The walk was slow but the pain kept her alert, focused on her destination. It was nearly dawn when she arrived at the waterfall.

The blue-gray light of dawn swirls and settles over the waterfall as black night fades. She has been to this waterfall many times in her young life, attended rituals honoring various Gods, but has never seen it in this kind of light, at this time of day. Never before had she noticed or appreciated such beauty, a kind of beauty not proscribed by tradition, the kind of beauty that seeps in beneath her pain and wraps itself around her battered soul.

She climbs the narrow ladder to the top of the falls, no longer in pain of body or spirit. The gentle rush of the subdued waterfall sings to her at the top and she stands on the platform, just above the spot where the river makes its heavy drop over the edge. The light becomes brighter, the waterfall regains its roar and its full muscle is unleashed by the light. Her head, never allowed much thought, is now clear, as clear and sparkling as the river water rushing off the edge.

She thinks of her nameless baby daughter, and how fortunate she was to have been sacrificed as an infant, to have been spared the life of a woman. In the blue-violet dawn sky, one bright light still shines, defying the efforts of the burgeoning daylight to overpower it. Rohini's daughter wasn't given a name before she was sacrificed, so she gives her one now: Blue Star.

She sings a prayer of blessing for her daughter, Blue Star. She sings the prayer again for herself. And then she jumps.

Days later, her body surfaces downriver and it is only then that anyone notices she is gone. Chatter was minimal. Her body was abandoned, she was pronounced a disgrace by her families and summarily forgotten.

When she emerged on my side of the Waterfall, I greeted her, made sure she was welcomed. She was happy to be welcomed into such a gorgeous place, where she would never be beaten, but she cried when she realized she would not find her Blue Star here. She wanders unsatisfied, drinks in the copious beauty of this world and worships the Gods she brought along, revels in the absence of violence, but she will not find complete peace.

There are Widowed Brides. Widows who destroyed themselves out of heartbreak and grief and widows who destroyed themselves because it was expected. Mandated. The ones who came here by decree don't understand the ones who came here by choice: *why*, if it was not expected of them? The ones who came here by choice do not embrace the ones who were forced and now, only the newer ones are still able to see each other.

Mirea was in love with her husband. He was a good man, he loved her back and they had a good life. Still young, they had big plans: material gains, higher position, children. There was plenty of time.

Things can change so fast. It was just a day trip, a waterfall hike just a few hours away, a popular spot swollen with spring runoff. A new camera. Home in time for dinner with the in-laws.

They bickered a little on the drive out. Stupid things, the everyday conflicts of marriage. It would soothe itself out by the time they got there, no doubt. At the park, the bickering continued, light, with veins of both love and irritation. The park was empty, every parking space was open and too many choices gave rise to too many opinions. She let him lead on the trail, staying silent and just a little bit behind, and by the time they got to the top of the falls, both had let go of their pique.

What a good day they picked to come to the waterfall. Always spectacular, it was even more so now, pumped and bloated by rampant snowmelt. It was almost frightening in its power, and they cautioned each other to be careful.

It happened so fast. Tempted too close to a wet, dangerous edge by his new camera, Mirea's husband slipped and disappeared into the water before she could reach. Screaming, she lunged for the edge. All she saw was one hand reaching out of the water as he went over the falls.

In the searing grief of the moment, time stands still long enough for her to realize that he will not survive. He is already gone. In that tiny stretched-out moment, everything flashes through her head at once: all of her history with her Beloved, all of their plans, all of their hard work and everything they will never be. Everything they will never do. All of the stupid bickering. The unrealized dreams. The rest of her life without him.

There is no one around to stop her, no one to pull her from the edge, nothing to contain the insane impulse of sudden grief. All she wants now is to follow him, and she does.

She wasn't surprised when she pulled herself out of the water on my side. She expected to end up someplace unexpected. But she expected her husband to be here waiting.

Where is he?

His was an accident, yours was suicide.

No! It was an accident, I slipped. I didn't mean to.

It doesn't matter. If it was an accident, you wouldn't be here.

She was not comforted by the chatter she left behind, relayed to me by the Boatman. Their bodies were found in the river, a few days apart and it was assumed both deaths were accidental. No one she left behind knows it was suicide. The chatter holds each of their deaths in equal esteem. An accident is just that - an accident - no one left behind has any uncomfortable thoughts about *why, how could she, why didn't we know,* no one is haunted by what they could have done to stop her. To rescue her from herself. The chatterers will always assume they are together forever, united by their love and their shared accident and they will take a degree of comfort in that. *So perfect for each other. So golden. At least they will have each other for comfort in heaven.*

No. She lost him forever by following him in. Here, *comfort* means *soft, undulate,* and it shies from her reach.

Abandoned Brides, overcome by a different kind of disappointment than Anniversary Brides. The love they vowed was forever was not. For some, it was a sudden and unexpected loss, not unlike becoming a widow but with the added pain of having to watch their lost loves move on without them. Some are left with responsibilities and obligations that are far more than one person can bear.

When Celestine was married, she vowed to make the honeymoon last forever. She smothered her husband with love and kindness and wifely manifestations of her love. She expected he would reciprocate, and he did at first, but soon fell into an everyday casual approach, without the daily frills. She tried harder, he resisted. She thought all of their time should be spent together - all of the time he wasn't at work - he didn't. She wanted constant displays of affection, especially in public, he brushed her off. Kept to the other side of the room. Her life-long honeymoon became a battleground.

It was all because she loved him, she argued. Why didn't he want to love her back?

Because your thirst is insatiable. I am running dry.

He left her with two young children, and she was destroyed. *What about **vows**?*

Done, he said.

He found someone new and she thought her wounds would never stop bleeding. She refused to let him see their children; they were her children now. *You left. You broke your vows. You're not fit to be around my children.* When a judge ruled otherwise, she was appalled, sickened. She refused to accept that a bad husband could be a good father and vowed to fight him to the death. She was soon bankrupted by her futile legal battle, and without any legal, moral or emotional support for her position and no means to continue the war. Abandoned not just by him, but by the world.

Sick with anger and righteousness, she takes her son and daughter on a drive, to a park with a famous and picturesque waterfall. She's been here before, with *him*. Before the children came. Before their marriage. Before he said, *Jesus, Celestine, do us both a favor and love me a little less!* The hike to the top is difficult with the little ones, and she has to carry them part of the way. Once at the top, she sets them down and takes their hands.

Wow Mommy, it's really loud! says the oldest, her boy.

Be careful, Sweetie. It's kind of slippery.

She holds them tight as she stares out at the falls, lets her bitterness boil up and churn like the whitewater pit down below. Sensing her unease, the children are nervous and the boy begins to cry.

She kneels down and takes them both in her arms. *No Sweetie, don't cry, see how pretty it is? See the rainbows down there?*

Come on, Babies, let's look at the rainbows. She stands up and takes one little hand in each of her hands, directs their gaze to the rainbows forming along the misty shore down below. She inches forward, they are hesitant. *Don't worry, I got you.*

They catch up and she inches another step, and another. *Don't worry, I got you. Don't worry, I love you.* Someone is coming up the trail; she hears voices behind her. A deep breath, grab tight to the babies' hands and she jumps, taking her babies with her to heaven, where they will be together forever without interference.

Among the chatter, the rage and outrage were immense. How could she do that to those babies? Her own babies? His babies? The people who saw her jump and drag her children with her were devastated by what they witnessed, and their lives were never the same. Publicly, they tried to blame her depression, which had obviously morphed into serious mental illness before anyone noticed. Privately, they blamed her - selfish, the ultimate act of selfishness. She always had to have things her way. He was a good father, she was too selfish to accept it. Bitch got what she wanted - now she has those poor kids to herself forever.

But she doesn't. As soon as she overcame her disorientation, she wanted her kids. *Why aren't they here?*

Because they didn't commit suicide.

Neither did I! I was taking them to heaven!

This is not heaven. I don't know anything about heaven.

If my kids aren't here with me, this is hell!

This is not hell. I don't know anything about hell.

Where are my children?

I don't know. I asked the Boatman, but he shrugged. He doesn't tell me where others go.

She will not accept that they aren't here, so she searches.

She inquires of those she can see. She tries to climb up the waterfall, undo what she did, but it swats her down. She thought there was hope when she found Jenny, but Jenny would not let her hold her and now she sees Jenny no more.

There are Deceitful Brides. Ruled by fluid moralities, various pathologies and other influential factors, women whose lives and marriages became twisted traps of lies.

Eliza never took any kind of responsibility seriously. She was taught to take what she could get however she could get it, and to shift blame away from herself at every turn. Raised to be corrupt. None of which brought her happiness.

And happiness was something else she had a right to take, however she could. Being of a materialistic nature, money and things equaled happiness; she had no real knowledge of any other kind. Eliza gambled; she won and she lost, she won and lost again, harder. Happy when she was up, it was the drug that drove the gambling, that craving for the happy winner's high. A happiness that wears off almost as fast as it comes on. She craved a happiness that would last, but didn't know what that was and the world was stacked against her. Someone else was always taking happiness away from her. It wasn't her fault.

She took others' happiness: money, things, other women's men, things that could be taken. She stole, she cheated, she was caught, arrested. It wasn't her fault, none of it was her fault, she was set up, she was framed, just more proof of how the world was stacked against her. With her smokey good looks and her gambler's wits, she charmed her attorney and the jury into buying her innocence and for a minute, that made her happy but like the gambler's high, it was fleeting.

It couldn't have come at a better time. Blowing the scheme for which she had been acquitted had cost her everything, and she was left in very desperate circumstances despite her legal innocence. Sensing a valuable opportunity, she turned up the charm on the attorney who believed in her and soon became his fourth wife.

But he was no prize. When his serial infidelities were

exposed, she was outraged - not because she loved him, but because she owned him. He laughed, bought her diamonds to shut her up and for a day, she was happy. The next day, she hocked the diamonds and took her favorite lover to Hawaii.

Then his cars were repossessed, and his creditors started calling her, too. His corrupt financial house was coming down around them. She had never stopped gambling, and had not felt the need to disclose this to her husband. When his money dried up, they received a very frightening visit from the bookie to whom she owed the most money. After tying Eliza to a chair, he beat up her husband in front of her. When the bookie left, her husband beat her up and threw her out on the front lawn, locking her out with nothing. Battered and bleeding, with nowhere to go and nothing to get her anywhere, she had to pull herself together and think, pull herself together and pull a massive transformational trick out of her hat *right now*. She was terrified, such as she had never been in her life - her husband said if he ever saw or heard from her again, he would kill her. When her gambling debtors figured out she would not be able to pay, they would kill her. And tonight's harrowing visit was only the first that she could expect. She wasn't even safe for the moment, exposed, unsheltered and vulnerable as she was.

She crawled away from her husband's front lawn and into the shadows of some bushes, until she could get her breath and swallow the pain enough to stand and stagger away. It's a well-heeled neighborhood, where the residents expect to be safe and some get sloppy with safeguards. She quickly finds an unlocked car to hotwire and speeds away, with no coherent thought of where to go. She needs cash to go anywhere, do anything and that can take more time than she has in the moment. The car she has stolen is very low on gas and she will be faced with the need to steal another one before she can get out of town. She doesn't have so much as a coin for a payphone. She hears sirens and panics - those can't be for her, can they? This quickly? She has to get off the main drag, turns without seeing where she's going and soon, she is lost. She still hears sirens - they were not behind her to spot the plate of a stolen car, so they can't possibly be chasing her. But her irrational mind takes over and her panic grows as the gas gage drops closer to the red.

Another siren bursts out, this one much closer. Not in sight, so it cannot possibly be after her, but she has to get away from it. *Now.* She grips the wheel as she frantically rounds a turn that puts her on a road going over a bridge. In the dark, she can't see there is a dam down below. The gas tank light is angrily flashing as the siren rounds the bend and is now behind her, flashing cop lights bearing down. She steps into a moment of defeat and floors the gas pedal, aims at the rail and blasts through.

The stolen car crashes down into the dam-controlled release of waterfall, slams into the concrete wall behind the flow and is shattered. She is smashed, destroyed, transported.

She awakens very soon after she arrives here, and with the knowledge that those lights and sirens were not chasing her, that car had not even been missed yet. The cops would have passed right by her without noticing her. With that, she is furious - convinced that her death was not her fault. She didn't do it on purpose, she wouldn't have done it had she known, it's not her fault!

Get me out of here!

She tries to grab me, shake me, but I slide out of her grip. There is no point in trying to explain anything to her yet. She argues that it wasn't even a real waterfall, it was a *dam*, it doesn't count. But manmade or not, it's still a waterfall.

She never found any heaven in her world and as she is, she will be even less happy here than she was there. Like Celestine, she does not accept that she is here, and she also searches. She interrogates and berates those she can see, and soon she can no longer see even them. She, too tries to climb up the waterfall, undo that which was not her fault, it couldn't be her fault, and she, too is swatted down. What she sees of this world has contracted tightly around her, as she refuses to accept anything about it, and can do nothing but antagonize.

I suppose that for the unaccepting, this could be hell. They can fight this for all eternity as they choose, but they don't have to. They can let go. Some do, some sooner than others. It is remarkable how this world changes for them when they do.

The Brides who come here do so because their marriage has somehow defeated them. I never married, I only dallied. Understanding their defeat is beyond my grip.

BRIDE STORIES

Rohini, who was expected and forced to be a mother only to have it taken away, tries to resume her pre-motherhood role of slave to others' needs. She knows she will never be a mother here - she has that degree of acceptance. Here, there are no men, and her only daughter was given to another God. Without the only structure she ever knew, she is lost. The rigidity of her life *there* has stunted her capacity for more.

But our needs here are not such that she can tend. She is shunned by those who don't understand her efforts and soon, they are invisible to her.

When Suzette arrived, many years later, she embraced Rohini. Before Rohini came here, she had no awareness of cultures that treat women better than she was treated. She was amazed that Suzette had been allowed to live so long without producing children. Suzette took Rohini's loss of her infant daughter into her own battered heart and together, they elevated Blue Star to their own Goddess and became her cult. Others have joined them, those who came here out of grief for their own lost children. Most have tried to embrace Jenny to fill their wounds, but Jenny will not have it. Celestine tries to join, but is rejected because she murdered her children.

Suzette, who bore no children in her time, embraces all of them as her daughters.

One by one, their demons take on the faces of their lost children. Only the faces. With all of their shapeshifting power, the demons cannot disguise that they are demons. The mothers reach with joy, then shriek with repulsion, turn back to the circle of their cult. Suzette enfolds them, strokes them, swats at the drifting faces. Ignoring Suzette's demons, they submit to her embrace.

Mirea and Celestine have embraced each other, feeding each other's delusions. Mirea, who knew her husband was unsavable when she jumped, maintains it was an accident, that she was trying to save him. Celestine maintains that she was trying to save her children, that she had to take their lives to keep them from a man they should have hated. This isn't right, they say to each other, we were meant to be together. He is here somewhere. They are here somewhere.

The more they search, the smaller this world becomes for them. I have wandered far and wide in this world and found boundaries I cannot cross, but what I seek is more nebulous, bigger. I accept what I cannot find here. They seek so intently that they are reduced to small circles. The try to climb back up the waterfall, where they are washed back down into the same state of confusion.

Their demons pose as creatures of light, taunt them with the means to light their way. It is their demons who trace the small circle in which they wander and search. It is the demons who step on their hands and boot them back down to the bottom of the falls. It is the demons who blind them to the realities of their chosen fate.

Celestine is haunted by the screams of her children as she dragged them into the falls and anyone who gets too close to her also hears them. They are horrible, those screams. Those screams *are* her demons, yet she insists that because she hears them, they are here somewhere. They are reachable. They are her children, they belong to her, they belong with her!

That's why I did this! For them! Where are they?

Murder, suicide, benefits no one.

THE SIGHT OF WATERFALL

Large or small, from the famous to the obscure and unnamed, *majestic*.

To see the sight of falling water is more than just the cold mechanics of water moving downward. It is the sight of transformation. Some of the water becomes mist as it falls, a wet moving cloud that never lands in the pools below. A much different impact. Waterfalls are shaped by rocks and chasms through which they run, sometimes broken into mismatching parts, even splitting into different falls. Never static, ever changing.

The small ones, the ones that look like faery kingdoms, they evoke calm and sweetness, invite you to sit, listen, make up stories you think you hear in the voice of the falls. Peaceful, and manageable. You can't get hurt here. The largest ones, the Niagras and Iguazus of the world, are too dangerous to be viewed unfenced. Careful distances must be kept.

There are other views from the other side of the waterfall.

The mood, the changes it makes with everyone who jumps in. The parts that shine, but only in the sight of those who *look*. The heave of the falls, the blur of my sight, and the metamorphosis. The opening of the portal to the sight of the waterfall from her side, the movie of her life, her head, her last day still playing as she tumbles down, already choked on the deluge, dying limbs sprawled loose and rag-like.

When she comes up again on my side, she still sees her own waterfall but I see all waterfalls.

Here, *majesty* means about the same thing it means there, only bigger. So much bigger. The absence of Gods here only magnifies the presence of *majesty, divinity.* The sight of the very first waterfall, created by Poseidon, was such as to redefine the words *majesty, divine,* and for the first time, I knew a level of *God* that far surpassed, dwarfed Poseidon.

Such is this Waterfall. All waterfalls. All Gods. One. Divine.

NEREID AND AMPHITRITE

I miss my mother, Amphitrite. Does she swim the seas looking for me, do the trails of her tears become currents of swirling grief let loose on open waters? I know that she knows what happened, but she's looking for my soul. I have immortal blood, I must be out there somewhere.

She doesn't know how final the act of suicide really is. Immortal blood or not, I am locked here forever, away from my mother. If she talks to the Boatman, implores him for information or visitation, he doesn't say.

But I talk to him anyway. *When you see my mother, tell her I love her. Tell her I miss her. Tell her not to come here. She'll never get away.*

He hears me. What he does with it is his choice.

My sweet mother, who never stood up to my father. He doesn't assist in her quest for me, he knows exactly where I am. His arms and mind are closed tight against me.

But she has forty-nine sisters to help her, who can swim every sea, every waterway, reach into multitudes of worlds. Do they? I don't know. None have broken through these barriers. I can only break through as far as the Boatman will take me.

She taught me to swim by strapping me to her back as a newborn, and diving into the sea. There was a moment of shock; even now, I remember it well. But it was brief. Once I was oriented, she unstrapped me and hovered while I paddled in awkward baby meanders, becoming at home in my element. It wasn't long before I swam far and wide, with her and without her.

I was rebellious. My father's fiery streak also lived in me and I chafed under his attempt to control me. He chafed under the need to control me. Amphitrite intervened by keeping us apart when she could. But it is hard to hide from Poseidon. On the other hand, the demands on a God's attention are staggering. There was plenty of time to escape him. And Amphitrite, meek and so unlike Poseidon, was easy to escape. Even then, when I still lived in her world, I heard her call me, felt her search for me when I was off their grid. But a girl must shed her mother's wings, and make the world her own. And Amphitrite's powers do not reach as far as Poseidon's.

I got into trouble. The blood of a Nereid and a God mixed in me to produce a trickster streak. Unlike my sweet-natured mother and forty-nine aunts, I could not always be counted on to be helpful. This brought embarrassment to Poseidon and turned his attention on me. His crackdowns were not pleasant. I strained at the bit he imposed on me, until his attention was diverted elsewhere and Amphitrite helped me escape. But he always found me, and each time he was angrier than the last.

I know there were lessons I should have learned. Keep my trickster under control. Don't provoke the anger of those more powerful than I. But the freedom and temptations of my fluid worlds engulfed me and I saw no need for discipline or self-control. When impulses lead to such fascinating things, what place is there for discipline? I was wrong to believe that the oceans were big enough to hide me.

Then, the waterfall. In a fit of blinding rage, he hurled a trident into a sea cliff, cracking it all the way to the river up above and Waterfall was born. All were stupefied by what he had done. He had opened a new portal between worlds and a new portal meant a possible escape. Eventually, I jumped.

And I escaped. Into a locked world accessible only by others

JENNY

A four-year-old decides she wants wings, the way one decides she wants a toy someone else has. Birds have wings, butterflies have wings. Angels and faeries in her baby storybooks all have wings. She wants to fly, to be like them, especially the angels and faeries, some of whom look a little like her.

Born with a craving for wings. Some cravings are born, not acquired, and those are the strongest. By age four, she knows all the winged creatures, real and imagined. She is especially close to butterflies, dragonflies, things that fly closer to the ground. Closer to her level. She knows she's an angelfaery, because there is no difference between angels and faeries. She begs her indulgent father for wings so she can be an angelfaery, and he responds by giving her costumes with fake wings that don't fly. When she cries for the real thing, he tries to deflect her craving by telling her angelfaeries aren't real but one day, a very long time from now, she will have wings when she goes to heaven and becomes an angel.

Where's heaven, Daddy? Can we go there now?

No, Baby. You have to die first. Remember, like when Great Grandma, when Toomah died? She was very old, remember? And when you're very, very old, a really long time from now, you'll get to be an angel too, just like Toomah. We'll all have wings when we're in heaven together.

But I want to be an angel now!

No, Baby. You have to wait until you're old, like Toomah.

Why?

Because we need you here with us! You have to wait your turn, it's not your turn yet.

Four-year-olds don't like to be told to wait their turn. The impatience born of craving eats at her and every time she sees something with wings, her craving grows. She pesters her father to tell her if it is her turn yet, her turn to go to heaven and have wings.

Her family becomes alarmed at her expression, which sends their sense of protection into overdrive. She is cautioned about danger at every turn. She does not immediately get the connection between danger and her desire, but she soon learns that dangerous things can lead to death and death is how you get to heaven, where you can be an angelfaery and finally have wings.

Her costume faery wings can't fly. At first, she is excited to get them - why all the fuss about danger and waiting until she gets to heaven, when here they are! Pretty, gossamer things, made from delicate, colorful fabric and decorated with sparkles but when she puts them on and cannot fly, she is inconsolable.

When her father takes her to see her first waterfall, she is enchanted. Naturally, she wants to be closer to the edge than her overprotective father will allow. She doesn't see danger, she sees rainbows, she sees a gushing ride to a giant frothy bubble bath.

Horrified at her naive analogy, her father blurts out that she would be killed by such a ride and a connection is made. She could die, *right here*. Right now! Right here is where she can go to heaven, where she will have wings.

It's my turn!

She slips her father's surprised grip and jumps. Jenny steps into a moment of craving and into the waterfall, arms stretched wide as if she already has wings.

Like the rest of us, it is the deliberateness of her act that brought her here, and keeps her here, regardless of her age and naivete. No matter the reason, no matter the age. Still, she is the only one here to get what she wanted by killing herself: wings.

When she emerged from the water, she was smiling, and lacked the disorientation with which everyone else comes through. She climbed out of the water, shook herself off like a puppy and looked behind her. There they were, dainty and stiff with newness, unfolding into the prettiest wings I have seen on any creature, in any world. And fully functional, the moment they were unfurled. With them, Jenny has passage to worlds no one else here can reach, yet this waterfall world is her home. It is whispered that she even has passage into the sleeping dreams of the family she left behind, but Jenny herself is silent on that point.

The chatter she left behind is simple, concise, and no doubt she also hears it. Four-year-olds don't commit suicide, they are incapable of such comprehension, such self-destructive intent, it is always, always, always an accident.

Yet here she is.

JENNY STORIES

Jenny, young and carefree as she is, is a little bit of a shapeshifter as if she is native to this land. The Boatman knows this, but others do not. Even in shift, I recognize her, and she does not shift for long. Cannot? However she shifts, she is still winged. It's why she came here. There is nothing she cannot do in wings. No one she cannot be, however briefly. She tends toward colorful faery-dragon types, bumblebees, miniature rainbow phantasmagoria. She plays demon, buzzes the others, lights ever-so-briefly on their hands, laughs and shifts away before they can see that it's really Jenny.

Jenny, young and unformed as she is, is already learning how to really be *diselemental.* She has a delight and an openness that no one else here has, not even me. She is afraid of nothing but the Boatman.

I don't know why he scares her. She will not say and he only smiles when asked. Maybe she thinks he has the power to take her away from here, to take away her wings, and maybe he does. Because I am his friend, she is also a little bit afraid of me.

Only a little. She will play demon with me as quick as she will with anyone else, always trying to fool me. But I always know it's her, and she flits away in a cloud of laughter, off to devil someone else. Never the Boatman.

I wonder what Jenny really knows, what she really comprehends. I hear the chatter, leaking through the portal she took to this world, as chatter does. The guilt she left behind has crushed her survivors, those who think they should have protected her. There have been two more suicides in her family, but none by waterfall. There, Jenny's death is not accepted as suicide and they have absolved her of earthly blame, but they will not absolve themselves. If she hears any of this, she shows no sign. Everyone here has chatter that leaks through the portals they took; most can't hear it. But Jenny, with her other unique distinctions, might also hear more than I know. If so, it is hers to keep.

The Waterfall is bigger through younger eyes, and in Jenny's eyes, nothing is bigger than the Waterfall. For Jenny, the immensity of it symbolizes the height and breadth of possibility, the height and distance she can go with wings, the very thing that gave her wings.

Jenny chases things the others don't see, can't see, some things even I can't see. Jenny once told me that ghost stories older than the waterfall itself walk among us, and I told her it sounded like something the Boatman would say. She looked frightened and winged herself out of my sight, and stayed away from me for months.

Here, *months* can't be measured in a calendar way. The boundaries of time are not the same. But they are still months.

Jenny once told me we were sitting on the head of another dimension, and she was waiting for it to sneeze.

Why?

Because, she said, it might make her smile. And if so, maybe it would make the others smile.

Jenny does not quite grasp the concept of drowning, despite her own drowning death. When she went in, she hit her head first thing and slept through the rest of it. She didn't understand about drowning before she went into the falls and doesn't know that she drowned. All she knows is that she jumped, what she jumped into, and now she has wings.

Her view of the Waterfall is different than others, different than my view. I view the Waterfall at eye level, and from below. Jenny views it from above. She flies high above and uses her

DRIVES

On those nights when the spirits are calm, do we gather around a campfire and bond? With the audio backdrop of the waterfall, that wet veil that wraps around and holds us all together, do we swap stories, mythologies, gripes?

There is no consensual community on this side of the waterfall. We are not One.

Some do bond together, in numbers larger or smaller, and some bonds last longer than others. Shared interests, here, often turn out to be superficial or unsatisfying and ultimately, misunderstood.

Collectively and individually, we wonder. I wonder who was the first one to ever commit suicide, by whatever means. Whoever it was, they are not here. I wonder about drives. With the survival instinct so strong, dominant, what drives some to destruction? I can only answer for me. Others might or might not answer honestly, because they might not know. Things do fade here, and what drove someone to act once, then, could be just another question here, now.

I question myself, what really drove me. Desire for something one will never have in that world. Escape from the inescapable. Here, only Jenny understands herself. *I wanted wings*, she says, *and I got them.*

A few wonder about me, some even ask. They know I was here first. They know I see all of them come through. What drove me? Some, even fewer, know about the Boatman. But that's all they know about me. They think I'm one with the Waterfall, because I was here first, they think it talks to me, reveals itself to me and it makes them afraid, makes them think I'm more than I am.

Much more.

But I drove here, too. As for the Waterfall, it speaks, but not to me. Whatever I hear is whatever it lets me hear, just like all the other voices here. Godliness and omniscience escape me here. Here, *goodness* and *mercy* mean flowers, magenta flowers, a certain shade of pink that grows only in the minute nooks in the rock faces of the Waterfall. Climb up there, and talk to those diminutive pink flowers about *drive*. What drives them? Even here, plants have roots; is the drive for moisture to survive the same here? Somehow, I think not....

Driven. *Pushed, forced, externally or internally.* I was born to a driver, I drove myself to escape him. I left all other drives in the Waterfall.

THE FEEL OF WATERFALL

You've touched a waterfall, you've hiked, maybe climbed to a pretty place with a picturesque, benign waterfall maybe not much taller than you. Maybe you swam in the pool into which it fell, swimming and standing under the flow to feel it pound down upon you, powerful and thrilling but not overpowering. You were never in danger of drowning or battering. Maybe you dove under it, if it was deep enough, felt the pounding of the falls the way a fish would: atmosphere pushed out of place, water disturbed by water. To the fish, it's just another current. To you, it's a tourist destination.

But when you go in hard, it's a much bigger waterfall. A much harder touch. No fish in the maelstrom into which you churn. The impact of the falls holds you down and you feel no more but you feel *something*, like nothing you have felt before. The waterfall feels different now, instead of holding you down, it opens up. Feel nothing, feel everything, feel one world become another, feel yourself go where only the waterfall can take you.

It can be cold in this waterfall world. Night comes when it takes a whim, weather changes on its own unpredictable cycle. There is no consistent measure of time. Time also has different moods on this side of the falls. There is no method of prediction or measurement, and no one here thinks to ask how long anyone has been here. The question makes no sense and there is no possible answer.

And it's not the same cold as is understood on the other side. The *alive* side. Here, *alive* means *elemental*. On the elemental side, cold is cold. Here, diselemental, all is fluid. *Cold* means *cold* and also means *fogged, thickened, obscured*. We feel cold here, it is elementally understood, but we are not bothered by it. It's not constant, but when it's here, it's welcomed by some, because of the change of mood. The clean feeling.

It can also be warm, but diselemental warmth is nebulous, weak. As there is no elemental need for warmth here, it is just another mood.

But what does it *really* feel like to go into a waterfall? It's not possible to live and tell. Elementally, the bodily sensations are beyond overwhelming and defy description. It doesn't take long to lose consciousness and when you come to, you are already dead.

But first, *immediately*
the crush of the force of thousands of pounds of water
all at once
smash you to rocky smithereens
and then a flash of a moment later,
you drown.

There is nothing peaceful, bucolic or graceful about it. You have thrown yourself into a meatgrinder of white-hot water-fire. Here, they have no memory of the pain of their flesh and blood battering. It stays with their dead bodies.

Isn't memory a sense? Take it away, and we are changed. When memory is gone, all there is is *present*, which is very confusing without the context of memory. There is no relevance. Without memory for comparison you don't know what you're feeling, touching, hearing. Doesn't that make it the very first sense?

Here, not all memories stay behind with your body. And they haunt, like demons. I see them down at the shore, trying to wash them out and send them back by the waterfall through which they came, or downstream, to still another world. Looking for a garbage dump. There, many had some kind of access to some kind of help out of their despair - they either didn't see it, didn't take it, or didn't seek it out. Or, it didn't work, because it was not the right kind of help. Here, there are no such resources. Whatever they brought with them, stays with them unless they figure out themselves how to exorcise it.

Even Jenny. As happy as she is here with her wings, she misses her family, and she doesn't understand why her great-grandmother isn't here. In time, she might, but she has no emotional role model, no incentive, no guidance. She's just Jenny with her wings. But Jenny doesn't spend time at the riverbank, trying to wash her family memories downstream. She has no regrets. She believes that someday, they will find her here. And who knows, they might.

No one here has yet been joined by a loved one who took the same way out. But who knows, they might.

They don't swim in their own Waterfall. But I do. Why not? It's home. The water, slippery-silky on my otherworld skin and scales, pulses with the power of the falls, and the movement of the river that drives them. Even here, the Waterfall is driven by the river. The river has no source in this world; you can climb to the top of the falls, if it will let you, but you can't follow the river from there. You can follow it from below the falls but you will follow it forever and never leave here. There is a source, and a destination, but it is not here.

Below the falls, the river fractures into tributaries, like blood veins branching out from a heart, mysterious passage-ways haunted by those looking for ways out. They flow every-where, they flow nowhere. They have their own inhabitants, most of whom are unrevealed until they feel the need to be seen, to escort someone out who has become too tangled in their pointless quest. I swim these waters too, but they are weaker, darker, than the Waterfall pool. They too are disele-mental, the waters and those who haunt them.

MARCASITE

On the day she went down the waterfall, she woke up knowing today would be the end. Not necessarily the end of her, but the end of something. It was enough to get her out of bed.

How to describe such a day? In the months, if not years leading up to that day, she started every day with the hope it would be her last but without a clear plan to make it so. On that day, she rose from her sleepless bed with a craving for delicacies within her reach, rather than the flaming hunger for what is out of reach. Simple things, little things, like an avocado on her scrambled eggs, a marcasite barrette in her hair. She felt satisfied, alive, almost beautiful, even though there was no avocado in the house.

She left the barrette on the rock at the spot where she went in. It had belonged to her aunt, who had gone out with a bottle of pills and would understand her leaving it behind, to be picked up by a stranger who would be unaffected by its history. Or snatched up by a greedy spirit with a love of green stones and glitter.

What a surprise it was to find she was still wearing it when she emerged on the other side of the Waterfall. Here, her name is Marcasite.

On that day, she drove through town, marveled at the easy

availability of so many things that one might crave. So many things designed and offered to satisfy superficial cravings. She bought an avocado and ate it plain, scooped it straight from the skin and sucked the creamy green goo from her fingers. Left grimy green smears on the steering wheel that quickly browned in the radiant heat of the bright blue day.

Despite her simple cravings, she was still without hope. There was no upwelling of love for life with the satisfaction of her avocado, or the sight of herself in the rear-view mirror looking attractive and mischievous in her vintage jeweled barrette. It was more of an emptying, like the need to empty her bladder before going to sleep. After she drove by shops, restaurants, bars, playgrounds of every kind, the absurd entice-ments of billboard ads, everything local civilization offers up, she drove to the waterfall, set her aunt's barrette on a rock and stepped in.

It was very fast. First, the power of the current took her to the brink, a power that is much stronger than what shows on the surface. She had somehow thought that once she stepped in, she would be able to climb out if she changed her mind at the last moment, but as soon as she entered, she knew there was no going back. The end she had craved for so long was upon her.

Then, the immersion as she went over the edge, sucked into the churning vortex of drowning, mouth and lungs force-filled with water and no chance to struggle, battered dead a split second later by the jagged cliff face behind the cascade, bones already pulverized before she hit bottom, forced down to the rocky bed by the unrelenting pressure of water pounding down upon her.

When she emerged on this side, it was with the feeling of passing through a long, oblivious dark. No memory, just feel-ing. She climbed out of the pool without help, awake and already dry, sat on the shore and looked at the Waterfall through which she came. Already, it didn't look the same, didn't smell the same. The sound was out of proportion to the size of the falls; then, slowly, the falls grew to fit the size of the roar. She didn't know a waterfall could breathe, but this one does. Inhale, exhale, it changes with every breath. This is when she finds she is still wearing the barrette. She touches it, recognizes it, orients herself to where she is and why. Feels the knowledge sink down through her, like a thick quilt dropping slow motion over her head and shoulders: *It really was the end.*

And now this, here. Oriented or not she still doesn't really know *what* this place is. For the most part, the Waterfall looks like it did when she went in, sometimes bigger, sometimes smaller. Sometimes, she thinks she sees a different waterfall, but she can't yet be sure. At first, she thought she would find her aunt here, because of the barrette, but she soon figures out that the only ones here have come by waterfall. She wonders if her aunt is in a place populated by pill suicides, and what that might be like. To each their own suicide hell? The things she imagines are not comforting.

She asks me, is this eternity? She knows she committed suicide, that she is dead, but what is *dead?* No one here can answer her questions. Some flee when they see her, some don't see her at all. She is confused that no supreme beings, no Gods or guides have presented themselves, that she has faced no judges. She can find no purpose in this world, no more purpose than the world she left.

MARCASITE STORIES

She was close to her, the aunt who took herself out with pills and left her vintage jeweled barrette behind. She looked up to her, wanted to be like her and when she was gone, Marcasite was bereft, lost and drifting with no one to reach for. No one to blaze the kind of trail she wanted to follow.

Her aunt's death was a shameful event, buried by the family with an unspoken pact to not validate her suicide by speaking of it. Marcasite did not speak of her pain, the family did not speak of theirs, and she was left alone with it. With her pain came intense confusion, and it is only now, here after her own suicide, that she sees her own confusion was the most intense of all. As close as she was to her aunt, her aunt did not confide her pain or reveal her intentions, leaving Marcasite to speculate and rationalize alone. When you are a teenager, everything is momentous, and without guidance, you are left to your own naive mind to make sense of the incomprehensible. She never heard the full story from anyone; it could be that no one else had answers either and silence was the only answer her family could offer.

Silent, they frowned when she wore the jeweled barrette. She hid it so it couldn't be taken away, then took to wearing it when no one was looking. With her aunt's jeweled barrette in her hair, she sat on the riverbank, tried to see as her aunt, tried to find her way into her head for answers. She pictured herself as her, riding in her old convertible with her curly hair blowing around the jeweled barrette, a comely but useless tool in the highway wind. But Marcasite's visionary head-trips provided no answers.

Her dead aunt became an obsession, she and the question: *why?* Her aunt had bouts of melancholy, but she also had bouts of bubbly joy, so why would she kill herself? *And leave me behind? I thought we were close, why didn't she warn me?* She didn't have a husband, but she didn't seem to want one. She didn't get along with her family, but who did? She yearned for things beyond her grasp - everyone does. Marcasite examined her own life, using her aunt's suicide as a yardstick for her own challenges. Applying her own reasons to her aunt's actions. She wasn't yet old enough for a husband, but she was starting to feel the pressure to marry. Like her aunt, she didn't seem to want one, either. She too had bouts of melancholy, but without the bubbly joy that her aunt showed, certainly not since her aunt died. She had felt nothing but deep sadness since her aunt died. She gets along well enough with her family, better than her aunt did, but she doesn't feel close to them. She supposes they love her, but do they? Does she love them? All of a sudden, she's not sure what that means. She yearns for excitement, which is limited for a proper young girl like her with an upstanding family, and she cries a lot, alone. There is no one else she wants to cry to. No one else to cry with her.

In her day, one kept one's true feelings to one's self, presented a composed and upright face to the public. The scandal of a suicide in the family was bad enough, it was her public and familial duty to show everyone that she, and the rest of the family, rose above it. To forget and pretend it never happened. The more she tried to buck up and forget, the sadder she became. She kept the jeweled barrette with her always, even when she wasn't wearing it, but she learned nothing from it.

Marcasite did what she did because her aunt did what she did. Such finality had to have been chosen for a reason, solid reasons, she told herself. Everything that went wrong for Marcasite could be applied to *her*: the same faces that turned her aunt away turned Marcasite away. The same doors were closed. The same wounds never healed. All links in the same chain. With no answers for herself, she could only apply her aunt's solution.

Assuming that all suicides go to the same hell, she fully expected to find her aunt here. Waiting to welcome her. But it was not to be and here, she is haunted. She can admit now that the strongest reason for her own suicide was to find her aunt, to ask her *why* and understand. Her aunt was not the sum total of her reasons, but she was the excuse.

Make no mistake, her aunt is not her only demon. The others buzz around her like psychedelic mosquitos but her aunt is absent, locked in her own hell, dominant by her absence. The negative space of her aunt's absence forms itself into its own demon, an anti-mirror image of her most loved one. There, Marcasite could conjure her up in her fantasy head and imagine that her aunt missed her, imagine that she promised to see her again, have deep, imaginary conversations which were only two voices in the same head. She could see her riding in the passenger seat of Marcasite's own little convertible, wearing matching jeweled barrettes in their wildly blowing hair. She could picture herself with her any time she was lonely and pretend it was real, but here, that ability is gone. The only thing she can conjure is her absence. Marcasite gained nothing by her suicide. What did her aunt gain?

CHATTER

Public:

Why? We never knew she was in such pain, why didn't she tell us - we would have tried to help; we would have moved heaven and earth to get her the help she needed

Why? She had everything going for her, we will never understand how she could throw it all away like that, forever

Why? Couldn't she see that her problems were temporary, she would grow out if it, doesn't every young girl go through this stage but they get strong and move on they don't kill themselves, why couldn't she

Why? He was in no way worth it, couldn't she see? She could have done so much better, somebody so much better would have come along, all she had to do was open her eyes and wait

Why? We only had her best interests at heart. We were just trying to do what was best. We always tried to do what was best for her. How could we know?

Why? How could we not have seen?

Why? It had to be someone else. Someone else gave her this heinous idea. She would have never thought of something so horrendous by herself

Why? Television. Movies. Music, kids today, such fatalism

Why? The books she read, the ones we found in her things, so dark, so Godless. Her diary, so much darkness on those pages, so little hope

Why? Where was God? How does He abandon one in such despair? We were always taught to look to God in times of darkness. Why didn't she reach out to God?

Why? They didn't mean it, they were just teasing

Why? Why couldn't she feel our love? We didn't know one heart could harbor such self-hatred

Why? How could he do this to her? How could they do this to her? How could she do this to herself? How could we do this to her?

Why? How could she do this to us?

Private:

How dare she?

Who better than she to choose when she dies - God ain't the one feeling her pain.

THE WATERFALL SPEAKS

When contemplating the feel of waterfall, do you ponder what I feel, tumbling down? Does my skin shred, do my bones break, do I drown again with each drop of water going down? Is there a rollercoaster thrill on the bumpier ones, a free-diving rush of the unimpeded plunge? As close as they might appear to describe, I don't understand those terms. How to compare the feel of blood bursting free from an opened vein, for that is what a waterfall is - a break in the river, an open wound. There is no pain in this metaphor, for I am the blood, not the wound, and blood does not feel pain. How to compare the pressure release of escape from confinement with speakable words? How to compare the sensation of separation of molecules into mist, as if I myself were losing blood, the reunification with the water, be it river, lake, or ocean at the bottom of the fall? How to compare the difference between the feel of **river** and the feel of **lake** or **ocean**? Comparison, empathy; there is no place for them, our touch does not overlap.

When the dam builders bring waterfall where there was never waterfall before, more than just the landscape changes. Water brings its own attendants, and the waterfall brings its own mysteries. Listen close enough to a manmade waterfall and you will still hear the forest, the winds. The smooth concrete walls do not compare to the natural cliff boulders, but rest assured the water will eventually erode all barriers and make its way back to a natural home, by one road or another. Eventually, the architecture of the dam will give way to time and a new natural site will be born. Time and water will ultimately erase all manmade things. But memory is not manmade, and its fade leaves a different scar.

The machine might make the waterfall, but it is no less defined by virtue of being born of a machine. It is no less **waterfall**.

Machines, dams, they are temporary. Water flows forever. Water will endure any and all constraint, containment, to evolve unbridled, to erode unrestrained as water will outdo

all restraints
all machines
stone and earth
to which
all machines
bow

And here, in Nereid's backside world, there is no need for dams, and my scars are easily washed clean.

In using me as a weapon of self-destruction, some come to me looking for baptism. Here, **baptize** means **strip away**. They come here thinking they have undergone the ultimate baptism, only to find so much has been stripped away that they have only their naked psyches for identification. In the world they left behind, the desire for baptism is strong, ingrained by ancient, entrenched legends. To be washed clean. The weight of sin is mighty, yet no one asks the waterfall if it can bear the weight of their sins.

I don't understand the word **sin**. There is no sin in my world. I know what others think it means, but that's not enough. I also know that their weight is their own, it cannot be washed away by me. Spiritual pollution does not taint my own purity.

Here, time freezes, thaws and flows, freezes and thaws again on its own notion. The souls who are lodged here feel it in different ways. Some liken it to seasons as they knew them, but it is not the same. There is no weather here, the atmosphere and its responses are not subject to planetary pulls and **time** as it is understood by them is a planetary thing. Cycles are planetary things. Dark and light, ice and fire are gradient and here, **gradient** means *flex*. Which is not to say that they do not feel November in their souls from time to time and somewhere, I will mirror that, show them frost and icicles like cold white lace. I let them feed on that until they are engorged with winter blues, bloated and ready to vomit, spiritually speaking of course, to purge themselves of their own private winters.

The flex of dark into light and back to dark resembles the flex of water falling from one level to another. Micro-droplets separate from the visible light and become flecks floating on their own air, rejoins itself at differing points or not at all. Light, dark, evaporate much like water.

Evaporation moves much more water than I do. Dark erases and light restores, light kills and dark buries. Different faces come into view. There are multiple moons here and they wax and wane unpredictably. The winged things flit back and forth, including Jenny, and stories filter back. Although these moons shine here, on their whims, they are their own worlds and there is no other overlap. The stories that come back by way of the winged things are about what they thought they saw, what was just out of their own grasp, not fully comprehensible by their own sight.

And what of my changing face, my own flex? Even Nereid cannot say she knows my every shade. In the eyes of the others, my face will never be more than they are ready to see, and they also have their own flex. Flex is powerful, unpredictable, a driving force in my world and not even Nereid can know her own. What they don't know is how I see and read their flex, how I know every change they make, conscious and unconscious. They will never know themselves as well as I know them, even Nereid, they will never see themselves and their reflections with the same knowing as the senses of Waterfall.

Man makes, but Waterfall will take away. A manmade waterfall will eventually be eroded and destroyed by the very thing it was built to contain. The Waterfall will decide where it flows, and if it flows over a manmade fall, make no mistake, the water has a choice. Here, some have built things akin to structures, but not quite structures, next to the water, in their attempts to reconcile themselves with their act and with their place in this world. They give names to their structures, to the water, to other things around them in order to integrate themselves and feel a part of it. They conflict with each other when one tries to name something someone else thinks they have already named, but there is no violence here, no name for it because here, violence has no effect.

Most do nothing that can be construed as pleasurable. But for Jenny, who came here before she learned about guilt, shame and self-hatred, and Nereid, who does not embrace guilt or shame, they see themselves as unworthy of pleasure. All of their feelings of worthlessness, uselessness and wretchedness followed them here, feed their demons and perpetuate their pain. Demons can be killed, but only by starvation. Only by the hand that feeds them. They see the beauty that is here, but they approach it with denial. Only Jenny and Nereid truly enjoy this resplendent world.

Though it is day and night here, some choose to see only one.

When their demon is guilt, they keep themselves in dark, believing it to be all they deserve. Cheat themselves of the light-time sublimity of this world.

Cheat themselves of the dark-time charms as well. Nereid and her Boatman know it well. They drink in the marvel of dark blue-violet glows tinged with green, magenta, silver, reflected off the water-ripples and bounced over the canyon walls, the scattered boulders and open meadows, under velvet canopy of what constitutes sky in this world. Skies like these, in worlds like this are the genesis of skies in the outer worlds. Here, **sky** means **blanket**, **rooftop**, and its stars are alive with their own movable light. They delight in the covert voices, whose timbres change and deepen from light-time to dark-time and all shades in between. They bask in the darkened scents of flowers that were pink or yellow in the light and are now scarlet orange, royal blue, glittery purple in the dark. They relish the moist softness the rocks take on in the dark, welcome the natural embrace of the cushiony ground when they lie down together. They luxuriate in the dark as they do in light, note the changeable details, compose poetry to compare the differences, dance to different music in each light.

For all of those who came to my edge and jumped, there are scars.

Can water sustain a scar? Here, **scar** means **duty**, and my duty to those who use me as a weapon against themselves is to channel them, funnel them into the proper hands.

Nereid's hands are far from full. Her scars are her own, theirs belong to them and mine are invisible to the human eye. Nereid wonders why there is only one boat on these rivers, but a better thing to ask is where they go, these rivers, where my branches grow and where my fingers really reach. In so many ways, she remains a child but she has eternity to reach and grow. She butts up against the boundaries of this world, the ones she has found, just as she did in her father's world, but as she grows, those boundaries will expand and she will travel even farther on my rivers.

Nereid knows how to swim among the low-hanging rainbows strung in the light-time mist. The others fear them, if they see them at all, but they are no different than the prismatic lights manifest the same way in their world. Here, on Nereid's side of the waterfall, these low-hung rainbow ribbons extend into the pool, under the waterskin, fluttering snake-like downward into the abyss. Bathe in them, wind them around your limbs, watch the colored lights split apart molecule by molecule, tickled with their vibrations.

Even in shallow water, there is magic, whether you chose to walk in it or over it. If you could walk in the mist, in the water that never reaches the ground, who would you meet? To enter this mist is to enter the waterfall in a different way than to enter it by solid water. Landscape, atmosphere is different in mist than in clear air or underwater. Those that live there cannot be seen, but they can be seen, but they can't be seen.

THERESA CATTERFLY

This one forgot herself on a lost river and found a waterfall. As soon as she saw it, all became clear. Unlike some, she did not wake up knowing it was her last day, or even craving her last day, but she knew it when she saw the waterfall.

It is the ego of Waterfall that creates the illusion of clarity. Nothing is truly clear in a waterfall, yet so many fall prey.

Prey is not the right word. The Waterfall does not hunt or snatch, it only falls and receives. This one, like so many, misunderstood. The Waterfall is always open to receive; the simplicity of this can be mistaken for clarity. In this pristine forest place, she felt her sadness lifted by the sheer force of the natural holiness that overtook her. It was a curious sensation, one she had not thought possible. Unable to attach another interpretation, she mistook it for clarity.

She never felt this much light, before coming out of the building and into the wild.

Suicide is not addressed in her church, so despite her ideations, she has found no comfort or guidance in church. Ones such as her need guidance for real, individual problems, not for the generic, global problems the church allows them to have.

There, her name was Theresa. Named for saints, but raised

in a denomination that does not believe in saints. It was enough to form a basis for confusion. Without consciously bringing the saint/no saint point forward, the confusing injustices of life and the resulting questions were such that she has lost the will to continue the struggle to untangle them. She is drained of strength and grasping at faith, but failing to find a grip. The feeling of drowning is so strong at times that she struggles to breathe. Pills, inhalers, prayers, nothing brings comfort or relief. Nothing brings change. Medical science pronounces her healthy, physically, labels her breathing problems panic attacks. Her religious parents wash their hands of it by telling her she needs to grow up and come all the way to Jesus. Only then will she really be able to breathe. She is doing this to herself, out of willful disobedience of God.

She prays, she cries, she questions and agonizes, but nothing changes. She is not transformed. Her struggle for faith is not lightened. Her church prays for her, but they do not know the depth of her struggles. The few efforts she made to unburden herself to her church were met with impotent responses that only made her feel worse.

Here, her name is Catterfly, because she is half caterpillar and half butterfly. Her suicide in the course of her quest for transformation has trapped her in a place of limbo, where transformation is suspended, never completed.

Looking back from here, in this natural temple of the Divine, what brought her to jump? Because every natural place in whatever world is a temple of the Divine. She arrived in mid-morning after a dour bus ride with her fellow church-mates, where young Christian spirits were kept raised by the singing of raucous hymns, with a focus on the upbeat. This is a *rally! Spirited!*

Theresa Catterfly wasn't feeling it. It was to be a weekend intensive of group activities and church structure, designed to bring them all closer to the church and its version of God. It was strongly recommended by her father (a self-proclaimed God-fearing man), by her pastor (the man her father wished he was), and others purporting to have authority to push and threaten and call it guidance. She gave in to shut them up, because she didn't have the strength to resist. She didn't have the strength to do anything else to help herself, to enlighten her own path, so the least she could hope for was that the relentless structure of the weekend would take her mind off of her real problems.

On the bus, hunched in her seat while her busmates sang bouncy hand-clapping praises, she kept her face to the window. The group sing only heightened the darkness she carried in her soul, a soul that was supposed to belong to God. *Listen to them*, she said to herself, *all in unison*. Lockstep. Robotic in their communal joy. The entire world is trying to turn her into a robot, and they think *this* is the cure for her ills.

The mood on the bus drops when they roll into *Amazing Grace*, everyone's favorite redemption song. It is the most sung hymn in their church, invoked to end every meeting, every gathering. She is confused, not sure how they went from hand-clapping to *Amazing Grace*, as the bus was still moving and the weekend was just beginning. She has missed something by not being tuned in to the group. It magnifies her sense of detachment from this group that professes to embrace her in the name of God, and from all else that the greater world at large tells her to tune into. How ironic that they are found, when she remains lost. Then they are laughing and she sees why: they are *there*. The bus passes through a gate with an arched sign proclaiming Lost River Camp and they have arrived. Lost River, maybe that's why they were singing *Amazing Grace?* It still didn't make sense.

Irony! The churchgoers are eating it up. She is close to tears.

After unloading and finding their assigned cabins, they are herded to a group welcome prayer and orientation. Standing in a circle with her fellow churchcampers, inside the camp meeting hall, a barnlike building with few windows, she is unmoved by the canned ministrations that are no different here than they are in the hushed air of the chapel back home. Maybe she would feel it more if she were actually outside in this magnificent natural place. She slips away and finds a trail into the woods, a welcoming place with an air of joyful mystery and the sounds of a different kind of hymn. It leads to a river - this must be the Lost River of the arched sign - and suddenly, she feels much less alone. They are lost together, she and this luminous wild river.

She follows the river trail, stunned and exalted by the beautiful forest all around, revels in the sounds of the river, the aqueous voices that sing and soothe. Voices that drown out everything but themselves and the breeze in the trees. There is no confusion in the river voices, no persuasion, just primal sounds of element playing upon element, water fingers strumming and drumming earth and moss and stone. The trail climbs a rising riverbank and crosses over a narrow wooden footbridge. Down below is a series of small waterfalls, fractured steps up the thick-forest mountain ladder. She is enchanted by the sights and sounds from the bridge and stands there for what feels like hours, drinks it in, fills herself with the majesty of the woods and the river and these petite waterfalls stairstepping down the mountain, undisturbed by anything, anyone. She has never felt so far away from the rest of the world, and she has never felt so at home.

She is entranced by the different voices of the river as it breaks over the series of falls. Sharper, more focused. More immediate. Edgier. After a while, she crosses to the other side over the rickety old bridge and continues to follow the trail as it winds higher, deeper into the wild. Her mind has never been so uncluttered. Her thoughts are without form or structure, and there is a cleanliness to them which she has never known. Thoughts that are visual, visceral; she has achieved a state of quiet, of being only in this moment, where the world is reduced to just her and what her senses take in around her. The landscape is dense, rocky green, earthbones laid bare amid the ferny forest growth. The trail narrows, more primitive, less groomed as she goes. Her feeling of envelopment grows with her clarity, fills the space left by the internal clutter she has shed along the trail. The river winds downward as she moves upward, snakes through the heavy trees on a track that is barely there, a way that opens just for her and closes, seamless, behind her.

The river song is stronger here, as if a choir of rivers awaits up ahead, behind a wooded bend. Her heart quickens and she stops to catch up with herself, to take it in, to hear a deeper voice that is stronger, commanding. Compelling. She follows the thread, loses sight of the river at several points, follows the ever-stronger riverbells, finds it again. The river reappears and the trail is re-established by another footbridge. She steps onto the bridge, out of the trees and is thunderstruck by what she sees.

Waterfall: tall, wide, magnificent, appears suddenly in front of her with a presence she can only describe as *holy*. She has never seen such a sight, never *known* holy. She has never been in the presence of such power. She has sat through countless sermons and bible readings extolling the power of God but has never felt it, never felt the presence of real God within her as exhorted by the sermons, the readings, the testimonies. She has reached for it, craved it, prayed for it, but it has eluded her.

And now, here it is before her. *Holy.* The full force of God. She is still in a blank-mind state, wordless in her thoughts, so God is not a word she puts to it in the moment. She is astounded by the pure force of feeling in the presence of the waterfall before her. The needle in her head drops to a familiar tune: *I once was lost but now I'm found* because that is the one word she can find for this: *found.*

Look what I found. Look what found me.

She stands on the bridge in front of the waterfall, mesmerized and paralyzed by its pristine power, its sanctity, its song. Its voice is more than the voice of a river falling over a cliff, so many more voices, but at the same time it is one solid voice. Yet she is not confused. She bathes in the cool mist of the massive falls, feels the weight of her world washed away by the light-fingered mist.

She has never felt so free. The sun drops and the daylight starts to wane, but she has no thought of leaving the waterfall. Before the light fades, she crosses to the other side of the bridge, where crude wooden steps take the trail upward, up the side of the falls. She moves quickly, hangs on to the trees on the wet, slippery steps, at last reaches the top where there is an old observation deck at the edge of the very spot where the pulsing muscle of the river dissolves into a churning conflagration that is alive with defiant force.

Without definition, she has never felt this way. Clear-headed and empty at the same time. The ionized charge of the mist clogs her nose hairs and paralyzes her olfactory glands. Below, small rainbows hang low over the churning foamy water, hug the rocky shore below and lace the low-hung tree branches as the sun gives a last burst of flame before it sinks into the coming night. She has stepped into a moment of ecstasy and she resolves never to step out. This is the transformation she has always craved; at the same time she feels its achievement, the craving for it flares out of control, a sudden hunger so gripping that she is momentarily blinded, momentarily deaf to the song of the waterfall, seized by such craving that she steps into a moment of abandon, crazed by the loneliness of the world beyond this waterfall, her waterfall. Once lost, now found. She climbs over the slippery rail and dives, arms stretched out wide to embrace the waterfall.

It will be days before her body is found. The time it takes her to come out on this side of the falls is not so easily measured. Catterfly, as she has now become, is still confused and like so many, angry that what she thought would be absolved by suicide rules her here, just as it ruled her there. The only clarity she has gained is the frustrating and irreversible knowledge that there is no clarity in a waterfall.

CHATTER AND DISTURBANCE

On her last day, Theresa's absence from the church camp was noticed around dinnertime. As it was nearly dark by then, the search was cursory, with everyone taking themselves to bed to puzzle over it until morning. Most slept soundly, as none were close to her.

In the morning, when she still had not returned, much nattering took place over coffee and scripture, with those in charge very displeased by the interruption of their well-choreographed weekend by a questionable member who dared to disappear. It was not until that evening that they decided to report her disappearance to the authorities.

Bloodhounds were employed and she was tracked to the deck where she went into the falls. Once they knew where to look, her body was found in due course, presenting new questions with the solution to her disappearance. What was she doing way out there? How did she end up in the river? It must have been a horrible accident. That trail barely there, so slippery in all that mist. Those old decrepit steps, so rickety, so dangerous. There should be a warning sign. People shouldn't be allowed to wander off alone. Dangerous. What was she thinking? The authorities questioned them heavily about her state of mind: had she ever threatened to do herself harm, what was she like, how did she act before she disappeared? *No no,* they assured the authorities, she was fine, never suicidal, perish the thought! No notes or other disturbed writings were found among her things. It must have been an accident. It's dangerous out there in those woods, alone.

But how did she really end up in the falls? They saw enough to question, and they didn't know what to do with the possibility of suicide in their church. They couldn't let themselves think about that awful possibility. Yet, she was known to be discontented, resentful, unstable in her faith. Unstable enough to....? It was unthinkable. Unspeakable. There are no platitudes for the unspeakable.

The coroner was not able to determine accident versus suicide, so it was officially declared an accident. Misadventure. That made them feel better, that let them feel sorry for her within their comfort zones. A voice of authority had spoken: It was just an accident. How very awful, but just an accident. No deeper implications, questions or complications. Nothing to disturb their faith, just more unknowable mystery to lay at the feet of God. Our hands are clean. God's hands are untouchable. Their devotion remains undisturbed by the struggle of Theresa, who is now Catterfly.

SLEEP AND DREAMS

Even the dead sleep and dream. Death can be as exhausting as life. On this side of the Waterfall, *death* means *river*, sometimes. Sometimes it means *flowers*, as in a field of flowers and all that it might contain. Because even here, flowers die; and just like there, they are reborn. And *life* sometimes means *peril*, or *canvas*, half-painted and unreconciled. Even here, sleep is the bridge in between.

When I sleep, my dreams are wet and mossy, with fog and sun competing to break with their various illuminants. Sometimes, I dream of grief, a drive that is shared between our waterfall world and the worlds left behind. They so desperately want to reach each other, those here and those there, and I feel their grief pressing hard against the veil, straining to break through and engulf their lost loved ones. And there are some here who craved that kind of grief before they went into the waterfall, who chose suicide for this very purpose. They don't feel the press of it as I do but they crave it, and grieve the loss of it.

The veil stretches and contorts with the weight, but does not tear. The veil will always stretch, it will never tear. Not even in dreams.

There is the Boatman, seen once in a while outside of my dreams but more often, within them.

Step into a moment of dream, where the Boatman's face is most clear. Beyond the boundaries of my waterfall world, there are rivers and there are dreams, confinement in and out of awakened states. He dips his oar in the silent water, but it is just for show. The boat glides on its own. I know I'm dreaming when I can't hear the Waterfall. I hear the fog, which is different than the Waterfall mist. The sound of it brushes against itself, like the unfolding of soft wool. The light tipples where it meets the water; the sound of it crackles at a slightly higher pitch than the breeze which rattles the trees. The boat glides silent, under the fog; the Waterfall is absent, and I know this is a dream.

A slow, narrow waterway, carved between rock cliffs older even than the Boatman. They are illustrated, but I do not recognize the hand. If the Boatman does, he does not say. Information does not move easily between the worlds, even in dreams, or from his lips. I trace the symbols on my skin, recording them to take with me when I wake, when they will either translate or they won't.

The cryptic symbols are now a map and I am excited, perhaps it leads to a different waterfall. I show it to the Boatman, but he is unmoved, and without this dream, I lack a vehicle to follow the map.

No matter, the map has forgotten me already and has moved on to something else. The skin I wrote on is blank again. The boat is empty but for me, and I know I am about to wake up. The map, the symbols - what little I remember of them - will all be meaningless in my waking-world.

The others sleep, and dream. It confuses them - they think of themselves as dead and therefore already asleep, why do they need to sleep? They pretend to remember their dreams, but they are disturbed. Perhaps they see the Boatman in their own dreams but cannot translate him into this world.

I ask him to take me along when he visits their dreams. I can see that they dream, but I can't see what they dream, where they go. If he takes me with him, will I see?

He does not acknowledge my question. Does not invite me to come along.

They are like puppies when they dream, moving their hands and feet as if grasping for something, running from something, running to something. They whimper softly, sometimes with tears, sometimes with smiles. I probably do the same when I sleep. Among those who lay on the shore, still unconscious from the battering of their suicide, some lay utterly still without movement or sound, dead in every sense of the word. I assume they, too will awaken one day, eventually. Just a short while ago, one who had been unconscious and *dead* began to stir. She is not yet fully conscious, but she is closer. Others, unconscious but not *dead*, also dream, restless in their minimal states.

Khamerina was unconscious for what could be measured as several centuries before awakening to this world. It took her a long time to orient, to come fully out of her fog and feel her feet on this moist ground. During that time she spent sitting on the shore by the Waterfall, she was still only semi-aware. Semi-awake. I sat with her sometimes, held her hand to give her some awareness that she was not alone.

When she was clear, when she could see and speak again, she told me her dreams while unconscious. For a very long time, she only dreamed of the Waterfall, her waterfall, of being suspended in the violent torrent of the falls. Trapped in the moment of her suicide, unable to breathe, yet unable to die. Eventually, the dreams became softer, and she was sometimes swimming freely in the dark, sparkling water, sometimes drifting uncontrollably, sometimes caught in something she couldn't define. On rare occasion, she saw a robed figure far off, standing in a boat, or on a raft - he was always too far away to be clear. She couldn't even say if it was male, but I recognize him from her description. The dreams became more abstract as she drew closer to consciousness, but the less she could grasp, the more it haunted her.

She understood she was dead. In her time and place, suicide was a rational, reasonable choice, but I can only think that something was wrong, something went wrong for her to be trapped in that drowning limbo for so long. Unable to breathe but unable to die.

. . .

They don't all stay unconscious for centuries. Some for years, months, weeks, as they can be so loosely measured.

One was unconscious for a few months, then was gone almost as soon as she awoke. Not gone, disappeared among the population of the others, but *gone.*

Gone from this world.

In her time and place, she was severely mentally disabled, with no grip on reality whatsoever. Whatever world her mind lived in, it did not overlap her everyday world. Confined like an animal, she was distraught and prone to escape whenever she could overpower her captors.

When she escaped, she simply ran, heading for open spaces until caught. One day she made it as far as the local waterfall, climbed to the top and jumped without thought or hesitation.

When her body was found, it was quietly buried alone, in an undisclosed place far from town. There was no further chatter. No one had a story to tell, for fear of resurrecting the horrible curse that had afflicted her.

I fished her out of the pool and laid her on shore and when it became apparent that she would not immediately awaken, I moved her to the sheltered overhang with the rest of the unconscious. She dreamed the whole time, making low guttural sounds, her feet moving in hurried little bursts, then still again.

I wondered why she was here. Was suicide really her intent? Did she even see the waterfall she ran into - did she recognize it as dangerous? Wasn't it an accident?

Somewhere inside of her, there was enough recognition, enough connection to form intent to suicide. Proof: here she is.

When her eyes opened, the transition was very sudden. She was up like a shot, running at full throttle just as she was running when she died. Wild-eyed, dysphonic, she ran erratic and circular, to the river's edge and almost in, then abruptly back and in the opposite direction. She ran straight for a flat cliff face jutting up near the grotto where the unconscious lie, and I expected a crash.

Instead of hitting the rock and bouncing back, she disappeared into it. I didn't even see it open for her, she was just *gone*.

Far downriver, almost out of sight, was the Boatman, standing in his small boat, leaning on his oar. Nodding, as if to say something wrong had been put right.

NEREID AND POSEIDON

A God must dominate, or he is not a God. A God must control, or there is chaos.

All Gods are not all-seeing, all-knowing. Most see, know far less than they feel is their due.

These are the cracks in which I tried to live and hide from my father. Sometimes it worked. When it didn't work, there was trouble. Amphitrite and her sisters, the original Nereids, grieved for the souls they were unable to save in the storms that were epic expressions of his anger.

His clampdowns fed my rebellion. He could lock me away, but eventually, Amphitrite found me and released me, seething with resentment and ready to rebel even harder. Once, he blinded me, but the gifts of one eye each from two of my Nereid aunts restored my sight. I left them safely on a rock before I went into the waterfall, to be returned to their generous and beloved original owners. Once, he cut me into seven different pieces and scattered the parts to the seven seas. Amphitrite and her sisters did not rest until they found and reunited all seven pieces and restored me with but the slightest scars. Slight, but still visible even on this side of the falls. Once, he traded me to the God Vulcan for a bottle of worthless wine that he said was at least more valuable than a worthless daughter. But Vulcan and I did not suit each other and I was uncere-

moniously returned. Amphitrite managed to keep me hidden
for nearly a year before he found out. Once, he cursed me with
electric eels, a horde of eels so dense and numerous and tight
up against me that I suffocated while the constant barrage of
their electroshocks drove me screaming insane. However long
I was forced to endure that curse - accounts vary - it rendered
me quiet and complacent for a very long time.

But not long enough for him. Never long enough, quiet
enough, compliant enough for him.

But of course, I loved my father. I loved my mother more; I
had more of a duty to him. It's just that I was no good at being
Daddy's Girl. By asserting my own dominance and control, did
I not honor the blood of the God floating in my veins? I didn't
want to control his world, I only wanted to control my own. I
only wanted to be lawless.

Gods make laws, Gods remake laws.

He can't reach me here.

He can't manipulate me here, lie to me here, punish me
here. Here, all I see is true. The others can only lie to themselves and still, they know the truth.

He loves me, like a father should, but he wants to rule me.
How else would a God treat his daughter? But I cannot submit.

Some lessons, while harsh, were valid. There are those who
see waters, salt and fresh, as treasure troves, and I am one.
Every boat that dips paddle in the water runs certain inherent
risks and sometimes, I was one of those risks. I was not vicious,
or bloodthirsty, but I was curious and sometimes, things got
out of control. For punishment, I was forced to ride with the
victims on their last journey across the water in the Boatman's
ferry, to hold their hands, to sit quiet while they pelted me with
contempt for taking their lives.

On these rides, I grew rich with witness. I held their hands,
felt all that they felt stream into me through our touch. Felt the
grief of their losses - not just their worldly existence, but all
that their lives contained that was beautiful, and worrisome -
loved ones, sensual pleasures, precious things; unfulfilled
obligations, lost opportunities and unrealized dreams. I felt
their last journeys, the ones I had disrupted so destructively.

Felt the blows as their vessels broke apart around them. Tasted the waters flooding their lungs. Died with them as they strangled in drowning. Some hands clamped me tight and others laid limp. Some tried to pull away, but I held tight, as mandated by my sentence.

Not all of them hated me for ending their lives. In those times, places, few lives were happy and some who held my hand were grateful for the end, happy to leave their misery behind and sail to a storied underworld. Reliving their tormented and hopeless memories through my hands, I wondered why they had not committed suicide. Hopeless, helpless, why had they stayed, waiting and hoping for something like me to take them away?

Not all on these journeys were sailors. Passengers, prisoners, innocents on fragile shores, unintended victims of my curiosities. I held their hands too, accepted their anger, contempt, or gratitude, and felt most guilty about them. Even the willing passengers don't know the full risks of the sea, like the sailors; prisoners and innocents weren't given a choice.

They all bore the marks of their deaths, bright scars and dark bruises that might or might not fade in the next world. I kissed the hands of each one when the ferry landed on the otherworld shore, told them I was sorry, hoped they would find favor with Hades. I did not ask for forgiveness.

Gods make laws, Gods remake laws.

Here, I am lawless, but I am also bound. Is it what I wanted? I can't say that I knew what I really wanted when I jumped, I only knew what I didn't want. Here, I am free of him, he is free of me, which makes me lawless, no matter how tightly bound. Whatever Gods are in control here, they do not show themselves. I do not feel their hands around my throat.

SUMMER BIRD

A most prolific waterfall. Gigantic, dominant, a magnet for ones who would worship it, pray to it, sacrifice to it, overestimate and underestimate it. The center of their world, for the abundant water that makes the waterfall also brings abundance to the people, and the power of creation and destruction is alive and palpable in this vast waterfall. One who went into this waterfall a very long time ago had this story to tell:

Her name was Summer Bird. Her people roamed this area near the falls for millennia, feeding off the rich green land with few neighbors and fewer threats, other than the everyday threats of the land. They came to the falls to fish, upstream and down, and to pay respects to the Gods who lived in them and provided the abundance on which they feasted. Summer Bird was named because she was born in the summer, and became most alive in summer. When she was a child, she could never be persuaded to sing in winter, only in summer.

For her, it was a hard existence. Her health was fragile. She suffered from asthma and severe curvature of the spine and often had to be carried when her people were on the move. Nevertheless, she was loved and tenderly cared for, but as she matured, she felt she was a burden on her people. The more she struggled to be productive, the weaker she became. As the elders often did when they became infirm, she stepped into the river and went over the falls. Following the belief of her people, she entered the portal to the next world.

The world in which she emerged did not match her beliefs, the stories told by the Elders about the place of the Gods. Other women of her people are here, but there is nothing of their world and in their confusion, they do not see each other. According to what she was taught, it was supposed to always be summer here, in her Afterlife, but there are other seasons here, erratic yet distinct and influenced by the emotions of the Waterfall.

Here, her name remains Summer Bird, even though she does not sing. If there is no true summer, there is no reason to sing. She has been here for a very long time and still has not found a season in which she can sing. Her voice, she says, lies with the stones at the bottom of the Waterfall. I would dive down and retrieve it for her, but there is no bottom to this Waterfall. Likely, it is now in the possession of a waterbaby, who will hold it until they are tired of it, then will leave it on the shore to be returned to her.

The chatter she left behind is kind, sympathetic. She was much beloved by her people and respected not just for her quiet suffering, but for the effort she made to contribute to the communal well-being. When she was able, she produced elegant, delicate designs on clothing and pottery, was always available to watch and teach young children and when she was feeling infirm, she did not demand, content to nurse herself to the best of her ability with the help of the tribal doctor.

She was respected for her last act, fulfilling tradition carried out by the old and the ill for time immemorial. They respected her for knowing when the time was right, when the deterioration of her condition was such that she could not continue to burden the people. She was feted and memorialized in the right ways and promises were made to her spirit that her story of brave suffering would always be told. They would forever be poorer for the loss of her sweet summer song.

But the nature of their lives did not allow for protracted grief. Survival was a daily concern, and the loss of Summer

Bird meant more resources for those who remained. But on late winter nights, huddled together in their dreams, they heard echoes of her summer song, far off and ghostly, faded from disuse.

They do not talk of these dreams; they are the most intimate, private part of a communal life and sharing is considered obscene. Dreams are shared only with the doctors, and only in the context of how they impact the people. But each one who dreams of her in this way mourns alone, without full grasp of the true meaning of *loss.*

CHATTER

There is also chatter in our Waterfall world. While not all who are here interact with each other, or with anyone at all, there is still chatter:

What is this world, why am I here, why is she here, how do I get out, is this all there is after death, this same fucking waterfall where I came in? I am not dead, how can I be dead, where is my family? I am not dead, how can I be dead, I didn't really mean to die
Yes you did or you wouldn't be here
but I want out, I need out, where is the God I revered, where is the door to this world, I need to find Him I need to find Her see I told you there is no God
there is no punishment either
Send a message can you please send a message my mother needs to know I'm okay
But I'm not okay
Why is this unlike anything I was taught why do these demons still plague me

They chatter too, the demons. Sharper; at the same time, quieter. This is how they sound to me - in the ears of their targets, the roar must overpower even the Waterfall. Nonsensical to me, because it's not meant for me, but much different in other ears. I hear their laughter, in variegated tones, but they are not laughing at me. I hear them singing, but I hear others singing as well. I hear their stories, and imagine how they sound to their intended ears. I hear drumbeats to accompany their poetic lines of chatter and I can't help but be drawn in. If it were not meant to be so, I would be kept in aural darkness:

See this mirror, your face is my own and the smoke that you blow
only makes things more clear you are but one in a parade bearing
tablets of ancient lines what made you think your woes would be left
on the shore? But we, your demons, we love that you brought us here
we celebrate the beauty the liquidity and fluidity of your chosen world
oh yes you did choose and we drink to that, your insane questions
only rattle your own blood suicide does not buy answers it buys no
entitlement
what are these demons that plague me
just you, just you, just you

EELS

Being who I am, I swim a lot. Few others do. Jenny swims, wings and all, but not as much as I do. The waterways here are tame compared to the oceans I used to roam, but they are no less unpredictable. And no less inhabited.

Despite my long time here, I'm still getting used to the emotions of these rivers, which grow from the states of the Waterfall. Currents and waves are not driven or bound by gravity, hemispheres, or atmospheres. Lakes have currents and tides which cannot be charted, which have no other source but the mind of the water, appearing and disappearing at will. Rivers are still, yet they move, they are vicious with undertow and lovingly calm, layered with oppositional currents and still currents on top of one another in shifting harmony. Colder, warmer, cooler again, maybe not for long, maybe for what your mind will measure as eons. Rivers, lakes, beneath the Waterfall itself, all of these waters allow me to swim. Most of them.

Even Jenny doesn't swim under the Waterfall, but I do. Here, there is no need to breathe air, which changes the experience in both large and subtle ways. In this world, the churning depth of the waterfall is endless. I swim deeper and deeper and have not yet found bottom.

The world I left behind was not devoid of the occasional

abyss. Hidden, secret craters and canyons, underwater and underground, dark and seemingly bottomless worlds all their own, they can be found in that world, if you know how to look. They are populated by interesting creatures and they hide mysterious things and some are devious traps.

Here, the abyss into which the Waterfall dives is largely inhabited by eels. Eel is the Trickster of our waterfall world. They are everywhere, not just in this trench beneath the falls which has no walls, no bottom, natural migrators who easily move from world to world. They are what you find by accident when looking for something else. Eels are dodgy, and they bite. They swim backward and forward, often at the same time, sideways and in and out of other worlds. They also have wings.

They are not as friendly (if that word can be used here) as other winged things in this world, and even Jenny shies away. The face of an eel is hard to look at for very long, as they culti-vate a look of malevolence as a means of protection and trick-ery. They bite, and I have been bit many times, as I am oblivious to their snarly countenance. They bite, latch on and shake their craggy heads, let go and ignore me. I am no longer flesh, I do not bleed, and I do not need to heal. Each bite leaves a little bit of eel in me, gives me a little more of that Eel sense of magnetic direction, which is invaluable in this world. I faced down flesh and blood eels in the flesh and blood water worlds, was bit and electrified, and I faced down far worse things than eels.

Here, they are the same, but different. Not just the wings, the wings are just for show. They don't need water to breathe, because here, breathing is an entirely different process than the traditions of lungs and gills. As such, they are also found out of the water.

Those who fear them see them more often. Looking for one thing, finding another. I see them everywhere, not out of fear, but because I go places where others don't venture.

Under the Waterfall, the heavy current presses downward for miles without weakening. Without stopping. The water continues to fall with as much force and definition as before it hits the surface of the plunge pool, the disturbance radiating outward through the surrounding water. In the abysmal depths, the light becomes more otherworldly and familiar sights are distorted. The eels change their shapes like the tricksters they are. Some become their own light source, prismatize their scaleless skins and reflect wet shades that are otherwise invisible, illuminate threadlike water-strands that would not otherwise be seen. Their stark, fixed eyes become circling stars, twinkle in halos rather than eye sockets, exponentially increasing their invasive sight. Their wings spread and deform, fragment and re-collect into waving limbs, antennae, shifting appendages reaching, touching, stroking, stinging. They shift into shapes of underwater flames, fountains, feathers, colorful variants and imitations of more solid things. They present themselves as portals with their enticing light shows, seem to wave and beckon you in, but to be fooled by this is to rush straight into their toothy embrace.

Their appearances stretch definition out of water as well as in. That thorny little wood sprite with the long fingers, he's an eel. They can't hide their eyes from me. Thorny little wood sprite eel swims like the eel he is, brushes up against me with ragged spines. Pull them out, and they become newborn eels, wiggling away into the shadowy depths. Bulbous body with short wings, trying to look like a caterpillar, he's an eel. Poke him and he snarls, emits an electric shock. They look like flesh and blood eels and they look nothing like eels but I know them. They have an undulate quality under their shifty shapes that betrays them as eels.

To me, they are more fluff than bite, because I'm not afraid of them. Fear only magnifies their power. Jenny doesn't fear them, but she stays away, doesn't go where she knows she will find them. I go where I want and shoo them away. Consequently, I get bit, but the damage I do to eels who interfere with me has been substantial. They cannot be killed, but there are eels who have been badly maimed by me and not seen again for a good long time.

The deeper I swim down the Waterfall abyss, the less aggressive are the eels. Here is where they get more colorful, formless. They are more curious than territorial, about this visitor from the surface world. As deep as I have gone, there are some who made even me wonder if they really are a portal, rather than a being. Down this deep, their embrace is much less sharp, but it is still the embrace of an eel and eels bite. Down this deep, their behavior is more free, less trickster. They spin, together and separate, lacy strands of wing, antennae, distorted wingfins enchanting in their deepwater dance. As they do in the deepest seas, they ball together, circling in, around and among themselves in dizzying spins and whorls, sometimes creating an underwater static that is as sharp as lightning, as if they draw power from themselves and their communal swarm.

Always, their eyes betray them as eels.

I am rich with witness

Where I came from, there is a land far upriver from the first waterfall and the sea, an isolated land long held by a small but contentious tribe, among other small, contentious tribes. It is a place where war was well known and the technology of war was highly refined in their Iron Age times. I stumbled into their land during one of my hideouts and witnessed a most spectacular, barbaric ritual to celebrate war.

There, too, was a waterfall, tall and narrow and easily accessed at the top. At the height of the ritual, when the crowd gathered below the falls had been whipped into a screaming frenzy, flaming matter was poured into the waterfall from the top, from huge boiling cauldrons decorated with fierce and bloody scenes. The narrow waterfall was lit on fire, a flood of flaming liquid crashing to the bloodthirsty screams and cheers of the populace.

I thought it was an abomination. I left their bloodsoaked land, rattled and bruised, and stumbled right back into Poseidon's net.

Here, the eels have somehow found their way to the top of the Waterfall. All day, I have watched as they appear at the top of the spill, slithering down the churning water with strange eely delight. One by one, they shift to fireflies. Each eel a perfect flaming, spinning firefly, small large and in between, filling the water one by one until they are all fireflies. Until they are one burning mass of firefly, of *fire,* something rarely seen in this world, gushing downward and setting the Waterfall on fire.

Abomination? say the Eels. Or just another waterfall on fire?

Under their shifted shapes, their deeper colors, the true eel shines through. They shift to this, to that, at brief random intervals, at their individual whim. There is rarely any kind of synchronicity in their shifts. They are never predictable. Here, *never* means *always* and many shades in between, but still *always,* still *never.* The eels flex their own shades. They are as contentious with each other as they are with everyone else, sneaky and territorial, bold and manipulative. They have mysteries of their own, inaccessible to the likes of me. It's not easy to see them shift. They are secretive by nature, more so when in shift. They use it to shock, jumping out as spiders, crows, demons, startling those who were looking for something else.

They shy from the Boatman, but he offers no insight. Eels, he says, they're too tangled for your tired mind.

One day I am with the Boatman, riding the river in his boat. He is amusing me by fishing for eels. Gonna take them home for dinner, he says, eel pie is an ancient delicacy. He fairly smacks his lips as he describes it.

And these trickster eels are going to take your bait? Then what? They're not killable.

Oh, they're killable, he says, but refuses to tell me how. He also refuses to tell me what he's using for bait. Whatever it is, it works, and soon he has five or six of them squirming in a wicker creel, from which they can't shapeshift their way out. He will take them home and kill them later, he says, cook them up right.

I try to picture his home. Where exactly, how, does the

Boatman live? Does he live alone, isolated, or in community? I don't need to consider how he kills those eels, that would drive me even crazier than wondering where he lives. As he says, a tired mind. And maybe that's why he's fishing, Trickster fishing for Trickster, whose purpose is to twist heads and tails, and to bite and spin when I get too close to its teeth.

EEL STORIES

S uch is the unexpectable way of eels, that there is one here who worships them as her God. In her oceanic island world, far from my own, eels were sacred, plentiful and protected. Her Eel God, the offspring of Sand and Water, pushed the primeval sky up from the earth, so that light and creation could emerge. The movements of her eels caused the rivers to flow.

Hers was a land of uncommon tropical splendor, lush-green and water-rich. Waterfalls abounded, large and small. She was witness to the arrival of bearded conquerors from foreign lands, witness to the rape and decimation of her people and land, witness to the eradication of their Gods in favor of the church of the conquerors.

Always, she had felt a special affinity for the eels. They curled through her splayed fingers dangled in shallow waters, visited her dreams and whispered blessings in her eager ears. She learned the songs and rituals sacred to the eels and invoked their protection whenever she went near the water, in the same prayer inviting them to swim with her. But her idyllic world could not be sustained against the conquerors. Villages fell, and resisters were driven into the island jungle, pursued and cut off by the conquerors until they either surrendered or died.

She chose to die. At the top of a straight-drop cascade, she made her stand, chanted the sacred songs of her eels and faced down the conquerors as they drew closer. Just before they could reach her, she turned and jumped, arms thrown wide to be embraced by her Gods. The conquerors fished her body from the water, battered by waterfall and eroded by fish, and put it on horrific, blasphemous display as a warning to other resisters.

When she emerged in my world, she found it similar to her own view of the afterlife, but was puzzled by its mutability. When she saw the eels, she was happy, believing that this is indeed her paradise. Still, she is confused by the unexplained absence of her ancestors and loved ones - surely they must be the eels, as per her beliefs in life. But why are they eels and she is not? Why do they not welcome and embrace her as one of them? Somehow, she must be unworthy, but she doesn't know how to become worthy.

She swims with them, sings her old sacred songs, endures their bites and shapeshift-teasing like an obedient child. She seeks them in her dreams, but the way she dreams here is different than the way she dreamed there, and the two cannot be reconciled. She seeks the same familiarity with these eels that she had with her eels, but these are not the same eels.

In time, she has confined herself to an isolated pool that teems with eels who enjoy her worship. She keeps her ancestral songs and rituals alive, and the eels respond in an oddly submissive way. They are still tricksters, but perhaps recognizing her sacrifice, they are gentler with her. She fears the wilder ones, outside of her carved-out corner, the ones who chase and shift and bite. The ones oblivious to her worship. Here, her name is Ri-iki, after her God, the God for whom she died rather than submit to a god she didn't know, couldn't see, couldn't touch. A violent, malevolent god who would never swim with her.

I know they move from world to world

Sometimes, I have dreams of my own about the eels. Here, the physical qualities of dreams are sharper, more electric, crackling with ionization. Ionization, the process that brings us here. It is in these dreams that the temptation to use Eel as a portal is strongest. What brings can also take away, just follow the conduction of the current. Eel will let you.

There is a connection, even in this world of convoluted connections, between ionization and the magnetic senses of the eels. Technical details are beyond my interest; as the Boatman likes to say, too much for my tired mind.

The temptations of dreams are legion... and eels feed on fear and desire bred of temptation. Certain currents are more visible in dreams, easier to catch and ride. Easier to get burned.

I tried it once, when I was young here, first getting to know the eels. I tried to take a ride on an eel current in a dream. I woke up bruised and burnt, battered by the barriers and boundaries imposed upon me in this world, and I couldn't remember any other part of the journey but the pain. Perhaps that was a blessing, a rare blessing from Eel. It was a mistake I have not made again.

They shift worlds like they shift shapes. They know my confinement here, and they come back to tease me about worlds I will never see. I don't have to believe any of it - I know Trickster's gift for fiction. They only truth to be trusted from an eel is that it is an eel.

So I shake off the dreams, and keep myself intact. If I am meant to move from this world to another, Eel will not be the portal. Each bite from an eel has heightened my magnetic Eel sense, enough to know Eel is not the way to anything good for me.

Another one here is the opposite of Ri-iki - where Ri-iki worships eels, this one fears them to the opposite extreme.

Born a frail, fearful child, she came up in a land wrought with superstition, with tales of eels arising from mud, dew, horsehairs shed in damp places, women's hair floating on water. She was plagued with nightmares of strangulation by the nasty, squirmy things and feared even wetting her hair in the bath. She avoided water whenever possible and could not stomach eating eels, delicacy that they were in her time.

It did not start, or end, with eels. Her fearfulness grew and spread, she could not stand to leave her house, could not sleep, could not tolerate the dark.

Then came war, and she was forced from her protective home. As a refugee, she was forced out of doors, with no protection whatsoever from her fears, from the brutal realities of war and the destruction of her world, with no tools, no means, no way to prevail and survive.

It was a matter of convenience, the waterfall into which she went. On her last day, she was beaten, chased, raped, beaten again, raped again. Already frail before the horror of war, she was but a crippled mouse in the enormous vice of her tormentors. When their backs were turned, she reached for an unknown well of strength and escaped.

Knowing her escape would be brief at best, she made the most of it. She headed for the sound of water and jumped. The waterfall was small, picturesque, but she couldn't swim and the water was swift and rocky. She was accompanied down the falls by eels, smelling vulnerability and an easy meal. Remarkably, in the midst of drowning, she remained aware of the eels, fighting them harder than she fought the drowning. Thus, when she came here, she was wrapped in eels, in shivering hysterics, fighting and screaming as they dropped off and slithered back to the water.

She is not at peace here. Her fears were not dissolved by suicide, and her demons are many. The most vicious of them look like eels - the snakelike eels from her past world. She has focused the brunt of her fears on them and has trouble grasping their shapeshifting ways. So taken by her fears, she has trouble telling eels from other beings.

Emboldened by the war that drove her to her death, she attacks anything she thinks is an eel. She tears at tree branches, looking for weapons, but the trees here are much more possessive of their limbs than the trees *there*. She picks up rocks, but when she throws them, they boomerang back at her. She cannot find peace with the amount of water in this world and she cowers from it, in fear of the eels.

The eels take no responsibility for her, and why should they? The ones who rode with her into this world have adapted quite well and aligned themselves with her demons.

It's the smell of a challenge. No trickster can resist, and another sign of the transcendence of eels. But even tricksters get bored, eventually. And when they do, maybe she will find some peace. As much peace as can be found among eels.

RIVERINE

The first time I saw the Boatman on this side of the Waterfall, I thought he was an illusion. I knew the Boatman well in my other life, that other time and place. But to see him here - *why is he here?*

Let's take a boat ride, he said. *Pack up your history, your drowning, your lack of faith and whatever else you have weighing on you and let's go.*

These are not the everyday words he says to the souls he ferries from life to death.

Don't worry, he said, *I'll make you leave it all on shore.*

Prehistoric, ageless, he wants me to believe he too has left it all on a shore so far gone and so long ago that he will have no sympathy for what I leave behind, or any tears I might think will tie me to it.

This is a different boat than I knew him to ply in the last world. This one is smaller, personal. Ornately carved with designs and symbols more ancient than he. Solid in the water. Comfortable, soft-blanketed seats for two.

I didn't ride that day. But that boat, it came back. Again, again, and again.

This waterfall world, it is not just a capsulized cubbyhole in a honeycomb of self-contained afterlives. It expands, contracts, shifts and floods, covers and recedes and uncovers new shores and meanders, islands and forestlands re-shaped, mountains a little higher, or lower, than before. The river loses its meander in the grasp of coming floods, silty overflow washes out and reshapes the dimensional land and a boundary that stopped me cold one day is gone another, yet it is still this same world. Another day came, the Boatman returned and this time, I rode.

Just as it is not that boat, this is not the river that connects life and death. On this river, *life* and *death* are not black and white states of being. This existence, in our waterfall world, is life for us now. It was our deaths that gave us this life. These rivers speak their own tongues, lazy diluvial tones cover mud-worn tales of other floods, shared histories of destruction and sustenance. Disguised by shifting waters, diluted by other voices riding under the waterskins. The Boatman dips his oar and the river voice adapts to his rhythm. A boulder vanishes and a tributary is revealed, fed by smaller streams trickling down through miniature falls. Such fingerling falls are just that: deep-rooted fingers of the one Waterfall, trickling out to tease. The tributary wanders into a cave and the winged inhabitants are not pleased by my intrusion, but are calmed by the Boatman's presence. Their clickety chatter sounds impatient, their yellowish eyes show restrained anger. Deeper in the caves, cathedral chambers drip and glow while the Boatman's oar creates spidery waves in the slow-moving current. The wake of his boat splits and braids the water like a woman's hair.

Emerge from the caves and the river splits, trisects, and the Boatman steers onto a branch from which I was formerly barred. Rainforest vines, tree canopies choke out the light, replace it with a violet-green glow. Here, the winged things are welcoming but wary. They have heard of Jenny, they evaluate her through me, scan me for what I know, what I have seen of her.

Another boat ride, another river branch, and we pass an enclave of Others who I saw come through the waterfall one by one from different times and places, but who subsequently disappeared. They are hollow-eyed, faithless. Faith, like life, is a liquid term and like these rivers, it has many branches, many streams, endless cataracts feeding a well that for these women, still runs dry. They spot me as we pass, running to the shore and silently pointing. Confused, I ask the Boatman, but he cautions me not to stop. They don't enter the water, stopped by a force that keeps them from wading in and reaching for the boat. Something coming from him, I am sure. I ask him, *Why show me this, if I cannot interact,* but he is silent, his expression closed. These rivers speak their own tongues, and the voices of these lost women have blended with the rivers, with the shrill scolds of their demons, with the fluttering wings of the eels, above water and below. The exclusivity of their language has locked them in place.

The boat moves on and the river narrows, wide enough for only the boat to pass, then suddenly opens out to a wide lake whose far shore is buried in mist. I hear the Waterfall, but I do not see it. The Boatman pulls in his oar, sits back to relax with his hands folded behind his head. From a bag he has secreted under his seat, he brings out a flask of very old wine.

Your mother sends her regards, he says. He does not mention my father.

It is the first time he has conveyed such a message. I sip his wine, fill my dry palate with old-world spices and a surge of unwelcome memories. Such pleasures are not available here, so this is a rare treat. Can the dead get drunk? I try downing the whole glass at once, but my throat rejects the imposition. The Boatman laughs, reveals a spark that few are privileged to see, as he refills my glass. If I am going to get drunk, it will be a slow process.

Other days, other rivers, but all originate from and return to the same river. A circular source. Each river speaks for itself, one water split into infinite drops. But each time I ride in his boat, he always returns me to this world.

THE SOUND OF WATERFALL

Large: the roar is oceanic. There is rhythm, pulsation, percussion layered under the roar. More under that, but lost to human ear. The roar drowns itself out, but the hypnosis of its voice seeps through. The sound of it batters through bones and brains to deeper cores, deadens fragile nerves and shatters what you thought was solid. Pure sonic power. Don't dare try to outshout it. It roars over you, through you, beyond you, reduces you to a single mind, one sharpened thought: *hear this.*

Small: it is the smaller falls that seduce with musical, friendly voice. Flirty tinkles and trickles splash and frolic in childlike bell-tones, autoharps and xylophones of the forest. Deceptive, showing minor magic to hide bigger truth.

Hypnotic at any octave.

Some say they hear its voice, that they are seduced by its song, they obey its command. Does it sing the same song to everyone - how do you know it speaks your language? Just because it's water doesn't mean that it's clear. How many voices make up that roar? How many different tongues? The collective voice of Waterfall is louder than any city, any war, and is even more heavily populated.

DIANA RASH

She comes kicking and screaming, trying to claw her way back up the waterfall as she tumbles down. The Waterfall has been heaving violently back and forth and I have witnessed a bitter fight with a man. A summer hike has turned ugly with escalating verbal one-upmanship. Whatever one feels, the other feels it more. Wherever one is wronged, the other is so much more wronged.

Her cravings are ravenous. Buttons are pushed, back and forth, harder and longer. Her heart bleeds. The river of her hemorrhage matches the roar of the falls but her screaming voice rises above it all:

I should kill myself, right here, right now, that would teach you.

And his: *Go ahead.*

And she does. As soon as she dives, she regrets. She is not yet dead but knows she will be, she has made the most grave mistake of all and she claws, she fights, screams into a chestful of water filling her with the force of a firehose.

There, her name was Diana. A strong name for a weak woman. If that is a harsh assessment, consider that she lived an impulsive life and she gave herself an impulsive death. There is little strength in that.

When she emerges on my side, she wants to believe she is

alive, that she miraculously survived her deadly impulse. But she knows. She knows, but she doesn't accept, so she jumps back in, claws at the boulders, tries to pull herself out of the water and climb back up the falls. She hopes against truth that the portal is still there, that there is a way back, that the strength of her regret is enough to save her.

But the eels who inhabit the crevices she grabs give no quarter, sinking sharp teeth into her hands. Desperation gives her no extra strength, not here. Here, *strength* means the same as it does there, but *weakness* means *deviation, derivative*. She tries again and again, but fails, insists that her impulse is reversible. Impulse or no, the intent led to the act and here she is. Here she will stay. There, her name was Diana, but she has been stripped of it here, renamed Rash. A more descriptive fit.

She struggles to forget, while she wears her history in her eyes. So many rash impulses, leading nowhere. Leading *here*. One irrevocable impulse leaves her here, forever? No one can say. She reaches backward and loses her grip, because there is nothing there. What she reaches for disappeared when she jumped. Her demons coagulate in merciless circles, chanting the last words she heard in her world: *Go ahead. Go ahead. Go ahead.*

Back in the world she left behind, the chatter has obscured her rash act. The man who urged her to go ahead has convinced everyone that it was a tragic accident, lest he be found culpable. But, his conscience is not entirely absolved and he drops hints of her impulsive act to others who understand, and his nightmares are relentless. His guilt will never die, as long as he lives and eventually, he moves away from everyone who knew her, to a town where he could be open about grieving a suicide, not an accident. The public chatter remains focused on the grief of the accidental tragedy, but privately, they wonder. *A life driven by impulsive emotion. She never really got hold of herself, never outgrew her childlike impulsiveness. She had a temper on her, that one.* They never liked that man she was with, could they be sure he was telling the truth?

Regardless of the real story, the whole story which they

RASH STORIES

Bewildering. An incomplete life, a bewildering death. A life lived (and died) by impulse is a life without maturity, direction, thought.

She is not the only one here who lived this way, died this way. Most suicides are rash acts, not usually the act of a reasonable, thinking person. Here, her impulsiveness continues to rule her and she rushes around, bumps into others who she should have seen, but did not. She hunts for other waterfalls, tries to tear them apart to reopen the portal through which she came.

Yet the Waterfall brooks no teardowns, no disruption or restructuring by any other than itself. She tears away the stones and they roll back into place, smashing her fingers and toes on their way back. She moves on to another branch, another waterfall finger, tries again with the same painful result. She tries again and again to climb the Waterfall through which she came, trying to reverse the irreversible. She is slapped down every time.

In her life, she was repeatedly slapped down by the consequences of her impulses and she repeatedly failed to make the connection between the two. Her moods swung high and low in radical ways but she was never suicidal, not in any kind of serious way. Fleeting thoughts only, not much different than most people, and never when there was a weapon at hand. Her relationship with the man who told her to *go ahead* was volatile, prone to nasty fights escalated over insignificant things, and with multiple breakups and reconciliations. On the day she died, their visit to the waterfall was part of a reconciliation celebration, but soon they were fighting about the same selfish things which led to the last breakup.

Here, she is still focused on the inconsequential; her method of avoidance. And here, she is free to avoid anything she can elude, but her demons do not make it easy.

Demons make nothing easy.

She demands sympathy from others, but there is none here to be given. *I didn't mean it*, she implores, *he made me. This is a mistake, have mercy. Have sympathy.*

But if she could hand herself some sympathy, it would be a step forward. She sees the Boatman and is not afraid of him - she swims after his boat, but he stays out of her reach. She believes he can ferry her out of here and maybe he can, but he won't. He also has no sympathy, yet he allows her to see him, as if the sight of him is part of some kind of punishment, or as if he is one of her demons.

I sympathize, but only with her discomfort, not with her fate. I myself was the victim of my own rash impulse. I am both comfortable and uncomfortable here and on those discomfited days, I too want to climb back up the Waterfall, tear it apart to find the portal through which I came and force it open with all of the power of the half-blood of my father. But unlike her, I worry that the portal could lead to a worse place than here, or worse still, back to the world from which we came and back into the hand of the mad God from whom I escaped.

The only thing she was trying to escape was an argument.

She didn't hate anything about her life hard enough to crave escape from it; she was not connected to anything enough to love it or hate it. Including the man who said *go ahead*. And like the man who said *go ahead*, she didn't love anything in her life enough to anchor it. It would have been just as easy for her to drift into any kind of not-so-accidental death because she wasn't hanging on to anything. The waterfall just happened to be the wrong place at a wrong time that could have been anywhere.

DENIAL AND REGRET

There are some, on finding themselves addled but aware on this side of the falls, who insist that it was not suicide at all. They were pushed, pulled, tricked, confused, and this is all a big mistake. They didn't really mean it. It's not their fault.

I don't know about that. I see what happens, and not just what is visible from her side. I see all hands, visible or not, all that would push, pull or trick and I see all the way into her pure heart, from her pure heart and her wishful heart all the way in to her dark heart. I see what really happened and things she doesn't yet know. Even as she asserts her denial, she knows that a hard truth awaits. But it is very deeply buried.

Others regret. A spontaneous act of desperation with irrevocable end and the magnitude of that momentary lapse is more than they can bear. They dive back into the river, against the current, look for ways to breach the Waterfall and return to correct their mistake.

They fail, each one, each time. It takes some much longer than others but eventually, most accept their fates. With tears, long streams of tears which return to the rivers and salt their moods.

But some smile. I smile. Jenny smiles, and Suzette. Others, but not many. Some find my smile disconcerting, others don't see me at all, but no one smiles with me except Jenny and the Boatman. But the Boatman is not one of *them.*

One, whose demon takes the form of a small green dragonfly with an old man's distorted face, smiled when her demon disappeared for an extended period. She laid on the grassy riverbank, arms slowly moving up and down over the velvety grass as if she were making a grass angel, smiling upward with her eyes closed. In time, her demon returned and her smile went away but when she did smile, it changed her.

Some of the demons are very smiley. It's part of their legend. The demons don't interact with anyone other than their own tormentees, and most others can only see their own demons. I have yet to see a demon in denial, or one with regret.

The rocks, stony boulders and cliffs that line the Waterfall and other waterways have faces, and names, and some of those faces smile. Not all turn their faces to be seen but even so, I can still tell when they smile. Other beings, all capable of smiling, none capable of regret. The eels: their macabre faces carry fixed grins, like the tricksters they are, but the smile of an eel is rarely genuine.

Here, *genuine* means *savant, characteristic.* The character of denial is directly prospective of the savant of regret.

THE WATERFALL SPEAKS

Nereid revels in her waterfall. And it really is hers, a secret gift from her father. This is why she is blessed with visits from the Boatman - he offers his friendship in homage. This is why she sees all who come through, their stories, their minds, their hearts and their deaths. It is not her burden to understand, only to receive. To curate. There are other purposes, but that is a higher level of understanding than either Nereid or I possess, that not even her father, the Sea God, possess. Nereid is her own concern, I am just the waterfall.

The Boatman takes her places she is not ready to wander alone, for he is so very much older than she. He watches, while she floats down hideout rivers, undisclosed creeks that only he knows, head-first downstream. Arms akimbo, it could be said that she resembles a cross, but she is no sacrifice as she slides easily down opaque rapids and shallow falls that are simple extensions of me, tasting the waterfall, smelling touching and hearing the waterfall, feeling the waterfall through closed eyes. Together we meander, we leave our imprint, our wet fingerprints on this world. Where the waterfall spreads, the boundaries change, and she will learn the boundaries of her own self before she will find the true boundaries of this world. Of the Waterfall.

Nereid is my legacy, I am hers. Sisters even, born of the same father. I belong to her, by the grace of greater Gods than her father.

Even Poseidon doesn't know that he made me for her, yet the Boatman knows these higher gods which Poseidon doesn't see.

*In the watery canyons of her world, littered with smaller falls that are still more of my own long fingers, blooming with rainbow greenery and crowned with canopy trees, she strolls easily up the steep downpours, trickles her own long fingers along jagged boulders and plush green moss. The hard-face rocks crack little smiles at the tickle-touch of her caress. The strums of my finger-falls echo up the narrow canyon walls, bounces and amplifies, fills the known world with my sighs and moans. Nereid, she hears me, she listens for me; of all the ones in her world, only she **hears** me. To the others, I am just background noise.*

*In the mortal world, water can be contained. Temporarily. In time it will revert to its natural state, unconstrained, and time is meaningless to water. **Water** plus **fall** means the power of water increases exponentially, proportionate to the height and volume of the waterfall. Man can make, and man can destroy, but water will outlast it all. Visit a dam. The smell of Waterfall, the sound of Waterfall, the feel of water, it will all be the same. Only the sight is off beat, yet not out of place in the industrial world.*

All that passes over my jagged lips is not the product of tragedy, but tragedy is the source of all myth. There is power in that too, but it is not I who chooses to use it.

The power I choose has more to do with shaping, not just the landscape, but myself as well. I am separate from the landscape, although the inevitable integration of landscape and waterfall is what draws. And so I will course, I will disappear, I might return, I might not. When I have chewed through this boulder and sent it crashing into my downrush, my face will be changed. You will see a different Waterfall, but Nereid will always recognize me.

*But does this portal change with my face? **Portal** is a very changeable term in any world. It has been said that when Nereid jumped, she opened the portal through which the others since came, but that oversimplifies and reduces a boatload of intricacies down to the lowest of human terms. Is there ever a complete grasp of any mystery?*

Nereid has learned much about the nature of portals since she came through mine. The Boatman helps her with that, in subtle ways she does not perceive. She remains bound to her world but her world is more vast than she has yet discovered.

From my view, I can look back on the path I have carved through the mountains and stone as I erode myself upriver over time. These women, girls who used me as weapon against themselves enjoy the same view from the shore on which they emerged. Their task, their struggle, is to apply themselves. Much is given up in suicide, turned away by those who need it most but because it belongs to them, it follows them here. Demons are merely what is most visible, because it was the demons that led them here, but they bring more than their demons. The Waterfall does not change who they are, what they need, or the power that gives it to them.

When they crawl, or are dragged out of the pool onto my shore, they still bear the bruises and battering of their death. These are not flesh and bone wounds, but they are none the less fresh and they will realize nothing until they fade. Each one carries a different burden, no less weighty than any other's; here is where they are to be laid down. There is nothing that can pollute or degrade my shores, these waters, this world.

From this pool, the tributaries of my river branch out and spread, watering forests and mountains webbed with trails, with bridges, with echoes of those who might or might not be reliable guides. Nereid knows many of them well and has mastered the riddles that pose as keys. It is not just because she is Nereid and this is her land, she gets very little special access. The same access is available to all who come here and want to embrace it, rather than fight it. The rewards are simple but momentous: tenuous degrees of peace with each key you are able to collect.

They would learn that the farther away they move from the orig-inal shore onto which they crawled, the more their view changes. Not just their view of me - they will always see me, no matter where they go in this world. Only Nereid can travel out of my immediate sight. The shores where they emerge are very cluttered, despite their lack of debris, and only by distance can any kind of clarity be gained. They can build here, in ways not conceivable in the world they came from, if they are not afraid to learn.

MINA

ina is reckless, doesn't care about her life in the way of those who want to die but don't have the final courage to raise an active hand. Despite her grisly openness about her death wish, it is important to her that her death not be seen as suicide. Suicide is for the weak. In her mind, a careful accident is not suicide, so she is reckless.

Her world: Mina loves animals but she loves drugs more. She hates people but cannot escape them, and drugs help her out with that. Drugs and animals are unconditional. And drugs can give her so much that people and even animals can't.

Raised by a cynical mother, she was taught to snap-judge and never waver. This trait did not serve her well; neither did it serve her mother and both refused to learn from this. Her life is not bad, by global comparison, but it is not what she wanted and she is disappointed. She has walked many roads; none have satisfied. She has embraced many things and been elevated by none. Her real disappointment is that she doesn't know what she wants, after so much exposure. She has searched and found nothing worth wanting, not with the passion she thinks she should have. Impatient, she has snap-judged everything without true examination or real thought and she makes her disappointment in life clear to all around her. She did not come from privilege, she was not taught how to find and exploit opportunities, only to snap-judge them. The ennui of disappointment has drained her of more than just hope, or of any desire to lift herself up. She is empty.

Out loud, she complains and wishes for death to solve her problems. She has a macabre sense of humor that makes others uncomfortable, some even worried, but they nervously laugh her off and tell themselves she wouldn't really....

Her head: She fantasizes, she daydreams. She plans her accidental death in a thousand different ways. At the end of her dreary days at the job she hates, her job of the moment, she returns to the home she can barely afford, ignores calls from those who are concerned about her and drugs herself into a more copacetic state. There, she can draw comfort from her imagined scenarios of death.

Death can only come as sweet release from her stupid problems and this deadly boredom. Released to what, she does not consider. In all of her imaginings, there is little to do with any kind of afterlife. She is not spiritual, she has no God, she can only picture a drifting oblivion, a state without needs or responsibilities. Free of people, free of need, free of disappointment. Released by a death that is not her fault, not by her hand, but the accidental hand of fate. Random, in the twisted way that being at the right place at the right time is random. Easy deliverance. Once in a while, she does something risky - skydiving, rock climbing, late night freeway drag races, and is disappointed to survive.

Does pretending for years in your mind prepare you for The Moment? When you hold suicide as your secret exit door, is there any such thing as an accident?

Here, *secret* means *blind*, the kind of blindness that is no accident.

Her suicide: So she is reckless. On her last day, she is rock-climbing with others - not friends, because that would mean that she cared about them, but climbing buddies. Others of reckless mind. It is a dangerous climb, up a cliff face next to a narrow waterfall. She has climbed with these two men before, knows them to be extreme in their thirst for thrills and trusts them not to care too much about her. Or to keep too close an eye on her. On this day, she has not consciously chosen it to be her last, she is simply indulging her everyday death wish.

They will take pictures of themselves at the top, standing on this waterfall that no one can reach but by cliff-face. But it is wet, the waterfall mist drifts all around and an already treacherous climb is made more so by surfaces slick with mist. She slips, a slight stutter before catching herself. Her heart pounds, adrenaline shoots through her like a needle-drug - *whoah, close! Close.*

How easy it would be. The release she craves is right her at her slippery fingertips. She laughs to herself and reaches for the next handhold but it slides from her grasp. She grabs, instinctively, but loses her balance before she can form any thought, tumbles down screaming, hits a boulder which sends her into the waterfall.

Her companions, both ahead of her on the climb, are startled by her screams. Instinct turns their heads away from the concentration they need on this dangerous cliff. The first one loses his grip and falls, knocks the second one off balance and sends them both down. No one survives the day.

In the seconds before she loses consciousness, she knows it is her death, and she knows it will look like an accident, however reckless. Just as she always wanted. She also knows it is not an accident, that the path she took to this moment is clear.

She is disappointed to be here. It is not the blank oblivion she thought she wanted. It is a continuation, a bastardization of the life she left, except she cannot stage an accident here. And the demons, they are no better than the people she hated. They wear the faces of those who loved her, but for whom she felt only contempt, but they do not show the same love. If she had known it would bring her here, she would have stayed away from that waterfall, that day. Stayed on to wait for a better opportunity to try it, to do it right next time.

The men who died with her, because of her, they are not here. Because they are men? Because their deaths were not suicide? Mina has never questioned.

RECKLESS CHATTER

It was an accident, without question. The public chatter stopped there. But they all knew about her death wish. She was so loud about it, it could not be ignored in light of her accidental death.

It was what she wanted, was it not? But how could anyone really want that? Did that make her ill? Unbalanced? Should we have done more, gotten her help? She was so obnoxious about it, all the time, it was just off-putting. Which at the time, seemed to be what she wanted, but wasn't it a cry for help?

It is amazing how many cries for help are never heard until after the fact. In Mina's time and place, her society had devolved to a level of self-centeredness that I, settled in ancient ways as I am, find confusing. Yet, I can only speculate that if Mina had looked outside of, beyond herself, would she have killed herself? Maybe. Maybe even sooner.

But my speculations are worth nothing. I listen to the chatter, as that channel opens to me, and I pray it never closes. I am not judge, but curator. This is a land devoid of judgement.

Yet I did not leave my curiosity on the other shore. It undid me then, it keeps me engaged now.

SPIN

The Boatman has set my mind to spin by telling me the Waterfall has sisters. I want him to take me to meet one but I anticipate he will refuse, so I have not asked. I ask him to explain the difference between a sister of the waterfall and the many other, smaller waterfall finger-branches here, but he refuses.

There, I had more sisters than I knew. Those Father Gods, they get around. Here, I am a loner in a community of loners. I cannot help but be intrigued by the concept of sisters of the Waterfall. The concept is not as straightforward as it sounds, and he might not be telling the whole truth. I have learned that much from this Waterfall and its fluid mysteries.

Even *there*, sisters are complicated. And complications build and multiply with the number of sisters. So much entanglement and intertwining, roots and branches far beyond blood. Among my own clan, it is more about water than blood, because water is our blood and water is a completely different kind of coagulant.

It is possible that the Boatman was being truthful but intentionally cryptic when he whispered that so-called secret to me. If it was truly a secret, he would never have revealed it to me. He is speaking in code, as in *Sisters* as a code word for something else. I have no boat but I can swim, I can walk, and I do. I have found no other waterfalls that are not clearly a tributary of this same Waterfall. Nothing to crack his code. But I can't say I have explored the full limits of this world; there are passageways I have tried to enter, only to find myself back here, at my own waterfall, and when I try to find these passages again, they are concealed. Other places are findable, but instead of simply returning me here, they drain me of so much energy that I am unable to move further and have no choice but to return on my own. When I ask the Boatman if he can escort me to these draining places, he merely shrugs.

Other times, he surprises me with a circuitous route that ends on a river I have previously tried to swim, only to be blocked. I brace for the border, but his boat glides smooth beyond it, and I am treated to sights I have not yet seen. Different, yet similar to the landscapes and waterscapes of the rest of this world. Landscapes ranging from the mundane to the phantasmagorical and everywhere in between. Caves not yet explored. I beg to go inside, but he paddles slowly by without acknowledging my pleas.

I always ask; one never knows - one day he might say yes. Or at least explain why the answer is no.

Once while out with the Boatman, we passed the entry to a passage that I know as one that forces me back by draining my energy. I implored him to take me in and he did, to my surprise. As soon as he consented, I was frightened. Immediately, I felt the same energy drain, felt the bare brute-matter force of it being sucked from me. The Boatman paddled slowly on and my fear grew as my energy drained, but I could not speak or cry out. I could not move. The stone canyon walls enclosing the waterway loomed high and menacing, bending over the boat and flexing their rocky muscles. Hooded stone eyes were cold, unwelcoming. Having got what I asked him for, I could only wait while the fear and the atmosphere crushed me, until he decided I'd had enough. I lost consciousness before that happened, and woke up alone on my own familiar shore.

Whether these barred places have anything to do with sisters of the Waterfall, metaphorical or literal, I don't know. It's never up to me. They will reveal what they want me to know in their own sneaky and self-amused ways, and my head will continue to spin.

Later, when the Boatman has gone and I am tucked into a favorite alcove, the light does its slow violet/green dance, changing from light to dark. Here, it is never truly dark, simply deeper. Deeper. Like an aurora, the darker colors streak the sky, flutter and twist while all of us below make our own adjustments to the light. We do sleep here, we even dream, but more from habit and escape than from physiological need. Some only come awake at dark, roaming ghostlike in search of one thing or escape from another.

He told me the Waterfall has sisters, without telling me any more. He knows how this will set my head to spin. I know he smiles, alone with his cognac and his fire, or perhaps with friends or another lover, enjoying my gullible hunger. It makes sense - at the very best, this Waterfall is but one face of an even larger Waterfall, whose other faces preside over other worlds.

For what of the waterfall deaths who were not suicides? Who were not women? Others commit suicide by waterfall - they must go somewhere, for they are not here. The Boatman is not the only male presence in this world: some demons, eels, waterbabies, trees, rocks etc can be distinguished by gender, some cannot. But the others who came here by suicide, they are all female. Why the need to separate us by gender?

Men and others also commit suicide. For the same reasons? I am female, other gender mysteries are little known to me. And the others who come here, they know others in ways I never did, and never will, having led much different lives than mine. Others feel pain, I am acutely aware of that from having inflicted so much of it on men in the world in which I lived. After all reasons are broken down and reduced by individuality, pain is the common remainder. Male, female, other, many who die in waterfalls are murdered. Some by religious sacrifice, some by malicious intent. I can imagine different worlds for such victims, more if they are separated by gender. Religious martyrs/sacrificial offerings are backed by a common belief that such sacrifice is for the benefit of the whole. The intent is not usually malicious, although it has been known to happen and such intent would change the nature of the act from sacrifice to malicious murder. Wouldn't the victim then go to a world that receives murder victims? Or does the act of suicide alone mandate our separation from all other dead? Is the afterlife as a whole an infinite honeycomb of microcosmic otherworlds, separated, crafted and sealed for certain kinds of dead? What about suicide by other weapons - is there a knife world, a poison world?

Many nights are spent this way, imagining the landscapes, the atmospheres, the populations of such worlds. Each starts, ends with a Waterfall. I can only assume it behaves like mine when a new occupant is admitted. I can only assume the Boatman knows these other worlds as well as he knows my own. I can only think that in each of these worlds, one was there first. Do they see, search like I do? Were any half-God, like me?

When the light rises again, I sit on the shore, gaze into the Waterfall for answers. There are none. There is scant revelation in this world, only hypnotic voices and more leaves of mystery.

CLIMBERS

Some try to escape by climbing up and out of the Waterfall. Almost every day, another one tries, often the same one who tried yesterday. The force of the Waterfall is enough to keep them down. There might be nothing, nothingness, at the top of the Waterfall that keeps them here, there might be an impassable boundary to another world, perhaps even back to their world. Whatever it is, it keeps them here.

I climb to the top, then jump down, dive head first into the churning pool of the falls. I delight in this; others who actually see it find it perverse. When I'm up there, there is only opaque mist. I feel something more than nothingness, but I can't move into it or beyond it. But I am not interested in reversing my suicide, so perhaps that is why I can get up there. This world is far from boring, and my father is not here. I have no other needs. The Waterfall doesn't slap me down because I'm not trying to escape.

Determination is not enough to pierce this veil.

But they climb, sometimes they reach the top and they come right back down again. Tomorrow, they climb again, same result. Some try a few times, give up, some try and try, retreat to rethink strategies and come back to try again. Always with the same result. Retreat again, try again.

But there was one....

once

A very long time ago, when I was young here. She came here not long after I did, from a waterfall that was far from my prior known world. We had little in common.

She chose suicide by waterfall over imminent murder by gang rape, as part of the pillage of war between generations of tribal forces. Here, she comported herself with serenity and acceptance, and here, her name was Pacifica. She was at peace with her demons, treating them like ignorable housepets. Starved by lack of what feeds them, they acted as such. She had her grief, but it too was peaceable. She was not one of those who regularly tried to climb the falls, or prowled the borders, looking for a way out to the next world, or for return to the world they left. Here, she was safe and sheltered, untroubled.

Until a day when she rose with a different look about her. Even more serene, if that was possible. Her small, fuzzy demons were nowhere in sight. Saying nothing to anyone, she dove into the plunge pool, reappeared at the edge of the falls, which had suddenly slowed to a trickle. With expert movements, she climbed up the boulders and the cliff face in a few swift steps, reached the top and was gone. *Gone.*

The Waterfall erupted, as if to cover her tracks. No one else saw her go, and I did not try to follow. But for the one who fled into the cliff face, every other one who has come through since I've been here is still here. As for the one who disappeared into the cliff face, I don't know that she emerged into another, different world, if she was spit back out into another unseen part of this world, or if she remains imbedded in the rock, unable to go forward and unwilling to back out. She is just one more who is are harder to find than others, having retreated to enshrouded, resigned corners, but they are here. And some continue to climb, get slapped down, and try again.

THE LOST RIVERINE WOMEN

On a day when I do not see the Boatman, I set out on the river, swimming downstream away from the sight of the falls. I feel the presence of waterbabies, following me because they think I'm up to no good.

Here, *good* means *cohesive.*

I deny their assessment of my intent, but they do not care. One gets too close, trying to pinch my fins as I swim, and gives a painful squeal when I kick it in the face. If anything with sovereignty over me smells my intent and wants to block my passage, they will do so. The river branches in a way I think I remember, when we passed the hidden enclave of Others. The ones who have disappeared, hollow-eyed and faithless, who pointed when they saw me, the ones I was cautioned against.

If I was not meant to see them, then why did I? Why did he guide me past - did he not know I would see?

The river has changed since that day, part looks familiar, part doesn't. All but one waterbaby has lost interest - the one I kicked, who still trails several feet behind, waiting for an opportunity to bite me back. With a mermaid's ease, I swim the branches, the tributaries, see the unfamiliar in the familiar, the known in the unknown, looking for signs of that enclave.

Another channel opens and I swim in against the current. The water rushes against me, but there is otherwise no barrier.

The trees look more familiar here, some are carved with symbols I can't interpret. They must be here. The channel widens to another river, choked with reeds along both shores, where I hide to watch for them.

The way they pointed when they saw me was disturbing, I have not been able to shake it since that day. Like the symbols on these trees, I cannot interpret. It was not welcoming, nor was it hostile - I think, but cannot be sure. The Boatman kept them from approaching me but couldn't, or didn't, keep us from seeing each other. Their wide, hollow eyes betrayed a blankness, a longing to know *something* to long for. How bereft can one be, to long for everything and know nothing, even after committing suicide?

Submerged to my eyes, the reeds are good cover. I have forever to wait and watch, with no mortal bones to tend, no one tracking my whereabouts. There is no clock to tick.

There are eels, enjoying my stillness, reminding me I am out of place. It is difficult to disguise my scent underwater and they make clear that I cannot hide from them. Not for the first time, I wonder if they spy for the Boatman. They pick at me, trying to provoke an outburst that will betray my hiding place but I am more patient than eels and when they become bored with me, they go back to their own games.

Dark and light passes and I remember how meditative a long vigil in a water nest can be. In the early mornings, the early evenings, when the light and colors are most unstable, I hear echoes far into the trees, haunted voices in concert with the colorful night breeze. The eels hear them too; it makes them restless and suspicious, then they are gone.

The women begin to appear on the other shore, first one or two at a time, then more and more. They are all familiar; they come from all walks of their worlds, all ages, all stripes. Some cling to the young girls, as if they have adopted them as daughters. They are ragged, bony, ghostly. Their eyes have grown large and dark, deep empty pits begging to be filled with *something*. They make themselves busy, and I cross the river underwater to another reedy hiding place closer to their shore, try to see what it is that keeps them busy.

I know each one, I saw their stories at play when they came through the Waterfall. Here, in this secluded place, the Waterfall can still be heard despite the distance and the isolation from the rest of our waterfall world. How do they mesh together now, this way, with so little common thread? There is a Bride, a young girl barely into her teens when traded in a political marriage to a disgusting and sadistic man whose idea of marital relations was violent rape, night after night until she was pregnant. On delivery of a son, the rapes began again and she took the waterfall way out. She appears to have been adopted by an older woman with curly gray hair like a corona around her head, a woman who chose death by waterfall rather than face burning at the stake. They are sometimes accompanied by one who was almost a bride, so conflicted by the choices she was swept into and so terrified of making the wrong choice that she accidentally on purpose went into a waterfall. Several have been here a very long time, victims of infirmities in tribal times when it was more honorable to deliver themselves into a sacred waterfall than to impose their burdens on their tribes. Unlike Summer Bird, these women had not been cared for and loved by their tribes, theirs were lives of abuse and privation.

There are some from impoverished places, hardscrabble times, so backbroken from hard labor that they, like so many others, accidentally on purpose went into a waterfall. They too are all ages - some backs break easier and faster than others. They knew no other possibilities in life than their own grinding experience, no other luxury than death by waterfall. The youngest of these ones appear to have been adopted by older ones of differing but sympathetic walks.

It has not filled their barren eyes.

Some were victims of horrible diseases, who went into waterfalls to escape relentless physical pain, who have not been able to shake their disease even here. Of course, the disease is no longer a physical condition, now it is the shape of their demons, still wrapped around them in eternal struggle. These are ones who haven't accepted that there is no bodily ailment that is *not* cured by death, be it by your own hand or by any

FIRE

F ire is a rare thing in this fluidic world. There is no need here for the attributes of fire - heat, fuel, cooking, destruction to pave the way for regrowth.

There is fire, but light, fire, they are different here. There is no sun to produce light, yet there is light; there is no heat to produce fire, yet there is fire.

The role of fire here is to burn. Burn what? For those who are as unsatisfied here as they were *there,* those with need to desecrate their own flesh, fire is here. They can burn themselves without real damage, indulge a holdover craving without actually satisfying it.

Because here, as there, flesh heals; here, without permanent damage. There might or might not be a new scar, depending on their need for scars, but the flesh as it exists here remains intact and ready to be burned or cut again and again and again. The craving will never be satisfied, as it is largely a demon in its own right. The fire is here to satisfy, temporarily; what they don't see is that all they do is feed a demon.

Others use it for comfort, a false warmth at best. They huddle next to small fires flickering in stone rings, shivering with a cold that cannot be warmed by fire.

What fire, for want of a better word for it here, does not contain: warmth. energy. ruination. regeneration.

What fire (here) does contain: light. color. movement. illusion.

When I was spying on the Lost Riverine Women, I saw they had a large fire set back from the shore, like a communal cookfire. It was carefully tended by at least two women at all times, but I never saw what they fed it to keep it burning. I was fascinated - it was the largest fire I have ever seen here. Is the size and strength of the fire relative to the number of women in their isolated breakoff community, multiplied by their need for a fire?

Fire appears to act however one needs it to, but without completely fulfilling that need. She who holds it to her flesh does not feel the pain she expects, she who cradles it for warmth is still chilled. Me, I cultivate small flames for the pleasure of watching its fire-colored dance, tinged with other colors of water, ice, jewels. It is pretty, but lacking. Persephone, in her underworld chambers lit with candles, rushlights and a large stone fireplace, cultivated fires of rich depth and color, dancing with rich powerful flames and fueled by peat cut from underworld bogs, in colors I never saw in fires in any other world, including this one. Fire here is a pale copy by compare. Its lack of destructive force makes it into more of a housepet, a domesticated shadow of what was. Even its light is dim, thin, more of an obscurant that would trip you up rather than light your way.

Some have tried to build fires in the traditional way, using tree branches for fuel. There is no deadwood here, so they tried to break branches off the trees. I wonder what they intended to use as a spark. The trees were outraged at these assaults and retaliated by sending the suddenly strong fire after them instead. And the fire obeyed, whipping itself into a small conflagration that engulfed them, head to foot, holding them in its hellfire embrace for days, months, before the trees' tempers had cooled. When finally released, they were horribly dried out and brittle, shedding burnt bits of themselves as they stumbled toward water. Hoping to regenerate in the cool river pools, they immersed themselves, only to be set upon by arachnids picking and plucking at their raw limbs, and eels poking, nudging, spinning around them until they nearly lost consciousness again. Eventually, they escaped the water, which sometimes held them longer than the fire did, and it was some time before they were themselves again.

Whatever passes for *self* in this world. Whatever it is, even the fire, the eels, and the water cannot destroy it. Only we can destroy our *selves,* again and again and again.

SANADORA

ancer.

C In her time, a one-word death sentence. No cure, only pain, then death.

There was nothing romantic or beautiful about her life. Not hardship, most of the time, but hard work. All of the time. But that's just the way it was in her world, everyone had to work hard. No one had much.

Physicians and healers had an uneasy coexistence in Sanadora's world. Resources were thin and medical science was rather primitive. People who couldn't get relief from Sanadora went to doctors and people who couldn't get relief from doctors went to Sanadora.

When Sanadora herself had symptoms that her potions and herbs could not cure, she went to a doctor. *Cancer.* She knew about this kind of cancer, knew neither one of them had a cure. There would only be pain, and death.

Healers shouldn't get sick; according to Sanadora and her traditions, it was bad form. She prayed to her spirits, a miracle being her only hope. She waited, prayed; the pain grew, no miracle came. She kept her disease concealed from everyone, lest it affect her reputation. Her family saw there was something wrong, but when confronted, she blamed it on simple fatigue. She prayed harder, the pain grew, and she went back to the doctor.

He shook his head, told her it was only a matter of time, gave her morphine. The morphine dulled her pain, along with her mind and the rest of her senses. This did not go unnoticed by her loved ones, so she threw the pills away and braced herself for more pain.

One day she woke up with no use of her left arm and an alarming weakness in her left leg. The pain was fierce, burning, strangling. She struggled to her feet, past her sleeping family and away from home. She caught a ride with a fellow villager and persuaded him to take her as far as the local waterfall. She had work to do up there, she explained, special prayers and rites that can only be done at the waterfall.

The man nodded his head with understanding and no further words were exchanged. He left her at the foot of the path leading to the top of the falls and returned to town, where he said nothing about the encounter until she was noticed to be missing. Sanadora's business was her own.

She struggled to the top of the narrow path, dragging her left leg, stopping to rest every few steps. It took the entire day to reach the top and when she did, she was nearly delirious with pain. She didn't want to sit, for fear she would not be able to get up again, so she leaned against a tree while she fought to breathe and clear the dizziness from her head.

A woman like Sanadora does not clutter her head with complicated or confusing thoughts. Not because she lacks intelligence or insight, simply because there is very little gray in her world. What was left of her days? Rapidly increasing pain, infirmity, to burden and disappoint her people. No one even knew she was sick - although those close to her were starting to suspect – and her death would look like an accident. She had come up here for legitimate reasons, according to the alibi she had given to the man who gave her a ride, they would say that she must have slipped. Just another tragic accident in an inherently perilous world.

Leaning against the tree at the edge of the waterfall, struggling to breathe and collect herself, she is struck by the soaring wonder of this place, her world, for the very first time. The hard lives led by her and her people did not hold much space for beauty, yet the beauty of the natural world around them was astounding. She feels blessed to be able to choose this magnificent place for her death; at the same time, sorry to have to leave such a lovely world. With hope, she will be welcomed into an afterlife that is just as beauteous. From her vantage point, solid-wooded hills stretched out endless green, twilight fog forming at the treetops and coming alive with night spirits as they awakened. The sun was setting and the sky above the high treetops came alive with coloburst, bathing all she could see in gorgeous changing shadows.

She feels peace, she feels the magic of the conjunction of the sunset of this day and the sunset of her life. She says one last heartfelt prayer to her spirits, thanks them for the blessings in her life, thanks them for this incredible waterfall, this enchanting sunset. She thanks them for the strength to make it here one last time and begs them to receive her. She steps into a moment of healing and jumps.

Her fragile body suffers little before loss of consciousness, and it is not found until weeks later. The driver's story had been heard and they had searched, assuming she had met an accidental end at the falls. Finding her body confirmed what they already knew. Certainly, it was an accident.

She is grieved, her tender ways as healer are sorely missed. Because no one knew she was sick and dying, her reputation as healer remained intact and in time, became part of the local legend. A revered ancestor.

When she arrived here, she was burdened by the weakness of the body she left behind. Although no longer *body* in the sense that she had been, it took a long time for her to shake that weakness. Being who she was, she knew that she should, and could, and eventually she did. Even after she regained consciousness, she stayed in the alcove with the others who are still asleep, stroking their hair and singing soft, low prayers in their ears. I explained to her what had happened, why she was here (to the best of my ability), she nodded in understanding and went back to tending the unconscious.

After a time, she felt well enough to venture forth, wandering the land, returning to tend to the unconscious. But other than tending to ones who cannot engage, she finds few who will embrace her. She wants to heal, but she still shows pain and lacks understanding of how to heal *after* the Waterfall. She too, has demons and trust is not earned in the ways she expects. Despite her hope to be received in a beautiful after-world, she takes no more notice of the beauty surrounding her here than she did there. She has since gone to live with the Lost Riverine Women, who do not necessarily benefit from her offerings, but they do not shy away from her and that is enough for Sanadora. She no longer returns to tend the unconscious.

That is enough. She has found a way to be at home here. Many do. Others do not, and it is her struggle with those who do not that drove her to that closed sanctuary. If and when she drifts out of it, I will be watching.

WATERBABIES AND ARACHNIDS

Waterbabies are not like eels - they do not readily interact with us. They are rarely seen and therefore, a mystery. They are identified more by what they are not - *What is that? It's not an eel... it's not a shadow... waterbaby?* Yet they are a distinct presence here.

Others have seen them and seek them out, particularly those who lost children in their lives. Celestine, still seeking to reclaim her murdered children, is convinced they are hers. They run from her as they run from most everyone, as a murdered child would run from its murderer. But they are not hers. They are not anyone's. They run from everyone, even me.

It is not entirely accurate to say that they have their own trickster streak - they sometimes do things that smack of trickster, but their intent is more protective. Of what, is never clear, given that *they* are not entirely clear.

They are most often seen playing with the arachnids. They are not spiders, but *arachnid* is the only word for them. All spiders are arachnids, but these arachnids are not spiders. Eight-legged, most of the time, they live underwater in bee-like honeycomb structures on the rocky walls of the deeper underwater passages, made from a hardened substance which they create themselves. They are shy, but much more visible than the waterbabies, and nasty-tempered when crossed. Helena

Reaper once captured one, thinking its fierceness meant it could kill her, but once in her grasp, the angry arachnid simply collapsed into itself, small as a grain of sand, slipped through her grasp and scuttled back to the water. None have allowed her that close since.

Jenny fears them, she brings with her a child's arachnophobia and by extension, she also distrusts the waterbabies. Jenny, who sees things even I don't. I have seen the Boatman dip his oar and bring it up with a dripping arachnid dangling from the end, furious and screaming like a fiend. They are brittle-looking creatures, colored with intricate markings, patterns that throb and pulse when they are angry. He flicks them off, drops them into his creel, tells me they are a delicacy in certain worlds.

What worlds?

On that, he is silent. He offers a rare explanation for them, for both the arachnids and the waterbabies: they are purged, discarded demons. Not all that I see here belonged to those who come to this world. While they look and behave much different, they are essentially the same - different branches of the same species, as it were. Waterbabies are harder to see because they are older. Arachnids will eventually fade into waterbabies, but it is a very long process, the kind of long that is measured different than *long* in this world. Purged and abandoned, they have lost their need to torment and the contrived forms imposed upon them by those they demonized fall away like dried-up fish scales.

But the arachnids, they are catchable, eatable?

He laughs, a jolly and indulgent laugh like a father whose child has just said something ignorantly cute. *Not by you*, he says.

How does one purge and discard a demon? I ask.

He looks at me with eyes that say the question is too banal for a response, then pulls his paddle out of the water and shakes two more screeching, clattering arachnids into his basket, where they are instantly silenced. The basket is hurried back out of sight, into the shadow in which it hides.

Where are you taking them?

He smiles, small and cloaked, cocks his bushy eyebrows. He would like to tell me, but he gets more pleasure from not telling me.

But I like this new information. Demons can be *purged* and *discarded*. Abandoned.

By this same law, can they not be castrated?

Some complain to me about their demons, often without clear understanding of what these noisy pests really are. *Demons*, I try to explain, **your** *demons*. Some understand and are able to see them for what they are, others do not.

The ones who can understand, I now tell them: *Castrate your demons*. Of those, the more enlightened ones set off in search of a knife. The others return to confusion.

The Boatman also finds this amusing. *Have you castrated your demons?* he asks.

I have no answer for that.

Still, this fascinates me. I dive into the rivers, the lakes, deep down to the honeycomb lairs of the arachnids and hide, lay in wait until I think they have forgotten me there. Time passes, while I watch them in their colorful eight-legged water dances, spindly legs slowly folding and unfolding in and out of harmony with each other and themselves in spidery, balletic movements. After a time, the waterbabies come, first one, two, then four or five. They are transparent, ghostly outlines vaguely shaped like pudgy babies but there is nothing babylike about them. Even in their ghostliness, I can see they are very, very old.

They join the arachnids in their sublime, indolent dances, limbs touching, almost caressing. I can see there is some kind of exchange taking place, but of what, I do not know.

It is a marvelous and puzzling sight. They used to be demons. Are they still? Will they become demons again? I know little about demons, they were not so prevalent in the world I left behind, although some said I was one.

But I have demons of my own. I emerge from my hiding place, slow and unthreatening, but they are not fooled and in an instant, the waterbabies are gone and I am pulling angry, squawking arachnids from my hair, digging their pinchers out of my skin. I grab one and it shatters in my hands, its razor splinters cut deep with electric, burning pain. I let go, frantically pull the fragments from my open flesh, as each splinter grows into a new, whole arachnid. They come at me in exploding fury and I know nothing else until I awaken in the bottom of the Boatman's boat, throbbing all over with pain while he watches me struggle back to consciousness, a bemused look on his face as he sucks the substance out of a fat and glittering arachnid leg.

THE SEVEN

One summer, one place. Seven girls. One by one, they went into the waterfall for which their town is tourist-famous. Each left similar stories behind: trauma and unrelenting despair. Each was partly inspired by another, to varying degrees.

The scandal was heartbreaking, growing with each one that went into the falls. *This must be stopped*, said everyone, and it was put forth that the way to do that was to deny access to the waterfall itself. Hide the weapon, end the suicides.

But suicide is not driven by the weapon. And the town had no power to close the waterfall: that power was held by federal hands and not subject to local demands. Volunteer sentries were placed, but this was discontinued when the daughter of the most vocal and visible sentry became the sixth of seven to die in the falls. After the sixth one, the tone of the furor turned from the waterfall to the parents - if this sentry couldn't keep her own daughter safe, what kind of parent did that make her? What kind of monster? The focus abruptly shifted from guarding the waterfall to guarding the daughters, yet one more slipped through to be the seventh.

The chatter about some kind of psychic contagion grew to absurd levels, but the contagion stopped at seven. Private superstitions, deeply buried, broke loose and multiplied - the town was cursed, paying for some past misdeed with the lives of their daughters. But the curse stopped at seven. Tourism swelled and the town prospered from macabre-minded spectators hoping to witness number eight, but number eight never came. A new mythology was born, latched onto and fed by webs of conspiracy nuts, each with theories more outlandish than the others. But reality remained unchanged: seven daughters dead.

Who were the seven? The first was Bethany, age twenty-three when she went into the waterfall, age fourteen when she was brutally raped. After a shockingly short prison term, he tracked her down, stalked her, raped her again. She left behind a letter describing how she felt she had no place else to go to be safe. The uproar she left behind was directed at the criminal justice system, the waterfall weapon was barely noticed.

It was not a week before the second one went in. Age sixteen, another victim of rape. Six months before she went into the waterfall, she reported it to the authorities but was not believed, leaving the rapist free to torment her and threaten further harm. She knew about Bethany and referred to her in her own suicide note - if Bethany, who had been believed and who had sent the rapist to prison, was not safe from her tormenter, who was?

The third one was another victim of the man who raped the second one. Voices were raised, calling for arrest and conviction of this deadly rapist, joined by those clamoring to close off the waterfall.

The fourth one was raped by her stepfather, who was imprisoned for it, but she feared he would be released one day and that she too would never be safe. The call to close off the waterfall grew louder. The volunteer sentries appeared.

But they were not completely effective. The fifth one, eighteen years old with a history of mental illness only sporadically controlled, nearly took one of the sentries with her when she went in. She had been awake for three days and nights, unable to shake her demons long enough to fall asleep, and had taken too many pills to try to compensate. By the time she got to the waterfall, she was crazed with fire and adrenaline and quickly overpowered the sixty-year-old man trying to save her from herself. She threw him off and he stumbled on the slippery edge, grabbed just in time by a witness. By then she was gone, number five, right through their safety net.

The resultant tightening of that net, with increased sentries, failed to stop the sixth one. In her last letter, she described an unescapable sense of suffocation and despair over the treatment of crime victims in general in her community and despair over the dismal state of human suffering the world over. Ever since Bethany, she wrote, she had been looking toward the other side and now, after an epic fight with her mother, who was another bullhorn-waving waterfall sentry, she snuck through the barriers after the sentries went home, and jumped.

The seventh one was fourteen, tormented and homeless. She was not from this town, like the first six, but a runaway from eighty miles away. It was rumored that she had been living in the streets of this town for some weeks before her death, but this was not fully verified and the chatterers multiplied that to their gossipy pleasure. Not being from this town, some were reluctant to include her in their cluster, but seven is seven no matter how you count it.

Here, the Seven all know each other, but they don't congregate. Because individually, their reasons for going into the waterfall have nothing to do with each other, regardless of shared experiences and references to one another in their last words. Here, they know there was no contagion.

Bethany, the first to die, waited by my side to welcome the next six as they came through, one by one. As shepherdess, she helped pull them out, dry them off and orient themselves, helped them understand where they are. Once on their feet, with the fog cleared, they each thanked her and moved on, away from the Waterfall, away from each other, with their demons in tow. One, Dana who could not sleep, I saw among the lost Riverine women, her hollowed-out eyes still seeking something akin to sleep. Once the last of the seven came through, Bethany's work was done and I have not seen her since. The two who were raped by the same man, Cameron and

Anna, have bound themselves to each other, as if they still fear the rapist they left behind. Jeanna, who was raped by her step-father, moves about among others for a while, then disappears, reappears with another group, disappears again when that group disbands. She follows me sometimes, runs away when she sees me with the Boatman and is not seen again for a while. Cara, the daughter of the sentry, denies that she intended to commit suicide, an impulsive accident in the heat of anger doesn't count, she's not really here. Gloria, the stranger, has decided she is safe here, and has turned her demons into lazy, affectionate pets. Sometimes, she talks to me, shares stories of her tormented life in detached, bemused tomes. Once, she told me she visits the lost Riverine women to see Dana, because she too had been unable to sleep for three days and nights before her death. Sadly, Dana is still trying to learn how to go to sleep and when Gloria tried to teach her what she knew about how to sleep in this world, her words became a language Dana couldn't understand.

They are a collective of the uncollectable, more linked in life than after death, seven sewn together in a cluster-quilt by the mythology they left behind.

CHATTER AND MYTHOLOGY:
THE SEVEN

The chatter is merciless. A cluster such as this, so many in just three months, breeds all kinds of hysteria. Merciless on the families of the Seven, the ones who, it was said, should have stopped this before it started. Those being held responsible by the public voice were equally merciless, directing it back and passing it forward and sideways to anyone, anything else that could be blamed. Anything but them, because to shoulder the blame for such a terrible loss is more than any human or group of humans can bear. Add to that, the complicating factor of the last one, the stranger, she who was not from around here.

Some felt comfortable blaming Bethany, the first to go in. She unleashed something unholy and contagious with her selfish act. Sure, she had a cause, what happened to her was horrific, sure, but did she have to take so many with her?

So many who should have been saved.

But they were not saved, and now comes the *why not.* A mythology grows, just as it would have in ancient times and the seven are the unhappy spirits haunting this now-cursed waterfall.

And what is better for tourism and local economy than a *curse?* A haunted curse! Which, in the way of curses, brings hand-wringing, public and private venom and more merciless guilt. And the haunting - but it will not be until all loved ones with living memories of the deceased have died out before The Seven can openly be turned into commercializable ghosts. But evolution and erosion will prevail, and most people's bottom line includes the need to earn a living. There are just some ways in which human beings might never rise above themselves.

They chatter at their God: *Let us pray.* The public prayers are brief: salvation for the tormented souls of the waterfall dead, peace for the ones left behind. The private prayers will never be admitted, will never end. The church's embrace of the families of suicides is superficial, vaguely or even overtly accusatory, in contrast to their heartfelt embrace of families whose losses are not from suicide. For those, God has spoken. God had chosen their time, as was only *right* and *natural*. There is no hand of God on the ones who choose their own time, and the church wants no part in assuaging a pain that was not afflicted by God.

A mythology grows. First, interest is kindled in the historic traditions of the native peoples in relation to this waterfall: did they practice human sacrifice? How did they worship the waterfall? Because they surely did, how else to explain a draw that lured seven young women to their deaths? Did these indigenous predecessors choose their victims from the spoils of war, or from the daughters of their own tribe?

Whatever it was, it surely left something deadly behind.

But ancient stories can't always be trusted, due to generational and translational embellishments. And they are far from complete, as those who cared to research soon found. The more unbridled among them went ahead and filled in the blanks themselves. First, by speculation disguised as intellectual discourse, then the so-called psychics got involved, leading to a no-holds-barred interpretation of whatever stories popped into their heads.

Something Deadly Left Behind. The more twisted of them ran in the direction of underground art, created serials of outlandish and exploitative comics, graphics, pulp, etc. When word and examples leaked to the mainstream townspeople, the resulting outrage only salted the heavy wounds and broadened a deepening divide.

Others posited that the mere existence of an indigenous tradition of human sacrifice was enough to lure the unstable into the destructive. If it wasn't the waterfall, they said, it could have been a romanticized story of a local girl who killed herself with a gun, then no one would be safe around guns. Or a knife, or poison... it's the suicide itself that has been glamorized, made attractive for vulnerable young girls.

Giving the stories a power they don't really have and creating another vessel for blame.

Some gave that power to the waterfall itself. *Greedy waterfall.* An ancient hunger once fed, will rage forevermore. The draw if its grandeur masked a deadly curse, one that reaches out cold and misty hands, wraps around the feet of innocents and pulls them in. How else to explain such a sad cluster? Religious extremists fed on this myth as well: the waterfall gushed from the mouth of Hell. The angry parent/spouse/lover of an ancient suicide laid down a curse before taking his/her own life in grief; they reached out now for long-awaited revenge. A sacrificial victim who didn't want to die, still angry, screamed an eternal curse as she was forcibly hurled over the edge. An innocent crime suspect, sentenced to execution by waterfall, another eternal curse echoing in the consuming roar of the falls. A crazy person spouting revenge curses for wrongs real or unreal, possibly unrelated to the waterfall, targeting the waterfall for being beloved by its people.

Word of mouth, other media spreads the myth. Curses and their sources grew into animate spirits living in and beside the waterfall, and stories grew around them. Juvenile campfire stories that adults tell kids and kids tell each other, mutated and embellished according to the individual proclivities of each storyteller. Some even brought in a sci-fi element, the waterfall as portal to another dimension, a classic mythological theme. Such spirits must feed, they lure in their prey by targeting the weakest who come to the waterfall. *Be careful, stay away, someone knew a girl who went to the waterfall and was spotted by a spirit who fell in love with her on sight and vowed to make her his own. This lovestruck spirit went so far as to stalk her in her life and her dreams, luring her back to the waterfall - weaker each time - until he finally pulled her in. Be careful, they're out there....* Lovestruck, ferocious, insane, otherwordly; imaginations here are endless. If gathered all together, the spirits of these imaginations would make for a grossly overpopulated waterfall.

And of course, the presence of spirits doing evil spawned the need for exorcisms. Cleansings. They came from all faiths: organized, mainstream, fringe, from the highest profile of public acceptance to the most outlandish and obscure. They performed their rituals in public and in private, added their own spice to the growing legends of spirits and possessions. The underground art and literature seized on this trend, blew them up and fictionalized them in the most salacious ways, adding fuel to the already contentious social divide.

Some even claimed possession of the falls in the name of their religion: a small but vocal group of devil worshipers pronounced the waterfall an open gateway to hell and conducted public and private rituals to establish possession of the waterfall in the name of their devil. They were countered with threats and equally public cleansing rituals, again from all religious walks.

After a decent amount of time had elapsed without another suicide, the exorcists and the cleansers cautiously claimed victory. The devil worshipers rattled their own swords and the underground arts continued its sick and lucrative output. Some adopted yearly rituals of renewal of memorial and cleansing spells, and new traditions took hold.

There is also the influence of the Stranger, the seventh and last suicide. A stranger to anyone here, she came here unbidden and threw her life away in *their* waterfall.

(how dare she?)

She added an unfair burden to their compounded grief by her unwelcome intrusion and they resented the incursion of this stranger on their private local tragedy, as if it marred the collection. But for her, there would only be six. The question of *why here* was never factually answered, fueling her own myth in the hands of those creating and distributing stories.

She had lived on the streets, said the myth-spinners, she had escaped from something evil. Bad parents, obviously. A homicidal cult, possibly. A child porn ring, maybe. Etc, etc, etc.

Or, one more rape victim unable to carry that burden, drawn by the call of the waterfall.

They were afraid she would extend the trend beyond their town, that she was the first in a wave of outsiders that would flock to their waterfall, to commit suicide and perpetuate an unwanted legend, bring a greater contagion. They were afraid of a real mass hysteria bringing all the wrong things to their town for all the wrong reasons, forever tainting a natural treasure that was already ruined for the present generation.

Her suicide was barely noticed in her own town, or rather, the town where she last lived. She reminds me of the nymphs who threw themselves off sea cliffs, or turned into trees to escape those that hounded them, only to be trapped in foreign form. Here, she is unhounded, even her demons are small and easily ignored, too weak to disturb the peace of her escape. Her short life was a series of escapes, each into the arms of something worse than what she had just escaped. By her last day, she had lost the distinction between days and nights on the streets because day was just as dark as night. Stories of the waterfall suicides were filtering down to the streets and she was curious. She had never seen a real waterfall in person and she wanted to see this place where the local girls were committing suicide. She was not thinking of her own escape until she got there and was overwhelmed by the towering power of the waterfall, unlike anything she had ever seen. She wasn't prepared for it, and couldn't tear herself away from its sight, couldn't tear her mind from the stories she had heard.

Here, they escaped.

Dead is dead, she thought, having any hope of heaven beaten out of her, already living in hell. Some had escaped this way and suddenly, she wanted to be one. She stepped into a moment of liberation and when she emerged on this side of the Waterfall, it was some time before she grasped the fullness of her escape, the implications of coming out on another side of *something*, the fact that she is not done.

Were it not for the six who went before her, she would not have gone into that waterfall on that day, but she would have gone, somehow. The chatterers were right to be concerned about contagion, but only I know how right they were. Although the contagion died with her, their fear of *more* never went away and will remain always a part of the legend, always ready and waiting to be revived with the next one to go into the waterfall.

No mythology is complete without ghosts. Hauntings. Those closest to the seven dead are truly haunted: by questions, accusations, doubts, regrets, memories, dreams, hallucinations. All compounded by insurmountable grief.

Some would make the seven dead into ghosts, ghost stories about beings who bear no resemblance to the real seven beyond their names, reduced to surly water spirits haunting the cursed waterfall. Some ghosts have even lost their names, morphed by the storytellers into generic evil haints, hungry for young blood/flesh/minds, eager to pull us all into a shattering waterfall death.

Also haunted are the sentries. The ones who couldn't stop them. Their guilt took them apart piece by piece, thread by thread. A classic conflict - those who are driven versus those who would stop them. They were not comforted by the fact that those who are truly driven will not be stopped, not by volunteer sentries. If the waterfall is unavailable, a gun, a car, a cliff is. The only sentry who had to confront someone trying to go in was nearly taken along and he was never the same. The sentry who left the waterfall unguarded when the last one, the Stranger, went in, nearly took her own life in the same waterfall, only to be stopped by a couple of alert tourists. The sentry whose daughter went in left town after the funeral, to spend the rest of her devastated life in a flat, anonymous town where no one would ever know how deeply she had failed. Five years later, she accidentally on purpose drank too much gin over too many pills.

The pain of a suicidal mythos never ends. Only the living can perpetuate a curse.

MINIATURES

Springtime, snowmelt runoff. They appear in hilly crevices, trickle down in rivulets measured in inches, but with all of the radiance and power of *waterfall*.

Tiny as they are, they are suicide-free, but with their own mysteries. Some appear at roadsides, a fleeting gift to lucky travelers - flowing one day, dry another. Farther in from the roads, these dainty falls are gathering places, hosts to small, esoteric things. Just as you and your family might have a picnic at a pretty waterfall. These kinds of picnics are more musical, more nocturnal, I hear. I am not able to attend such parties, but Jenny is. She comes back and weaves delicate miniature instruments from living flower vines and blesses our world with music from another world.

Even here, there is meltoff, although there is no season. Cold comes when it wants, melts when it wants. I ride with the Boatman, walk the land and swim the waterways, and I hear their tender trickles revealing unseen nooks. Miniature enchantments, they are deceptive in their shallow depth. I have seen how these miniatures open up, babydoll versions of itself, twisting and hiccupping like the large one but opening to admit Jenny. I once tried to follow but slammed face-first into impassable rock. Another concealed boundary that will not be breached.

There is one that is particularly exquisite, that I have seen a few times. It reminds me of one in a hilly seaside forest near a river I used to frequent before I came here. Only a couple of feet across at its widest point, it sparkles down a low, rocky, moss-green slope in twists and turns like long low stairsteps. Even there, I saw the waterbabies who gather along its brief shores, but who did not invite me to join. Here, they are much less visible to me, but I see enough to know that somebody gathers here.

It is not always here when I return. Sometimes Jenny passes through and takes it with her, and it does not return when she does. Then sometime later, there it is. Slightly re-formed, one part or another a little to the left or to the right of where it was last time, but the same elfin, exquisite waterfall, just as sparkling, just as inscrutable, still just another fluent finger of our one, only Waterfall.

Another one near the main falls attracts some of the suicides, ones who seek to understand themselves and the actions they took by understanding the Waterfall. Too raw to face the larger Waterfall, they cluster next to the tiny one, their way of reducing the magnitude of it all to a more digestible size. I don't know if it helps them; I have yet to see one of them move from the tiny one to face the real one. The waterbabies stay away from this one, Jenny stays away, but the eels love to devil the ones who gather there, give them an eel's perspective by showing how they are magnified by the little falls. They shriek and fall back, nervously creep up again when they think the eels have gone. The process repeats, not right away, but unfailing.

There is another one so minuscule, it even dwarfs the waterbabies. I saw an eel curled up next to it, and it made the eel look like a dragon. Jenny tells me this one is too small for her to pass through, it pinches her wings and she's afraid they will tear. Still, they gather, shrouded but strong enough for me to count. No more than two or three at a time, enough to show there is something about this dollhouse-size waterfall that draws them, that it has something to give. Unlike some of the other miniature falls, it does not come and go, it does not move. Also unlike the others, I cannot get close to it. I can sit next to the others, put my feet and hands in them, but this one won't let me within ten feet. No explanation is available. Just another minute, ineffable mystery of water tumbling over rocks.

WHAT TO WEAR IN THIS
WORLD

Here, bodies are fluid, shaped primarily by the self-perceptions and wishful projections of those who wear them. Me, I wear the watersheen with which I was born, sometimes traceable as scales, sometimes as skin, leaves, or robes in the fashion of my time. Jenny wears her wings, her little child's body more babyfat than when she was alive, aglow with her contentment.

Others wear shades, veils, rather than things, because things too, are fleeting in this world. Some are veiled by a kind of cloak, faintly similar to something they wore in life, or the clothes in which they died. In the right light, ghostly traces of their old flesh and bones glow through, laced with the scars of their shattering waterfall ride, as if the shadow-shapes of their former bodies are held together by the colors they wear. Some are veiled by more of an aroma, or a soft sound, than a sight. Faces are always visible and clear, even the ones who have been here the longest. Body habilis might change and evolve and even their faces might change in ways akin to aging, but not explained by it, but they are always clear.

Pretty wears her tiaras, wraithly banners of beauty titles for which only she competes.

Helena Reaper wears black and gray, floating like the robes

of her Santisima, her scarred bones prominent as long as she has the energy to keep them alight. As in life, costumes, wardrobes, take energy to maintain.

Celestine wears her anger in colors of excremental browns, muddy reds and yellows fighting for dominance over each other. Her scent is strong, fiery, an aroma of burnt bones and too much cinnamon: death and desire in the same sentence.

Rohini wears the glow of her Daughter Goddess, bright blue silver/gold sparkle in light time and dark. Hennaed hands and arms are bejeweled with all that was denied her in life. Suzette, her cultmate, is more subdued, in the muted shades of an acolyte.

Very few Brides wear wedding clothes. The ones who do are radiant and haunted at the same time, as if they are both enchanted and repelled by their status as brides. Their colors, silvery white when they are radiant, muted gray when despondent, slip and slide in and out of each other with their moods.

Catterfly wears the forest itself, the natural beauty of the true cathedral of her soul. She is often indistinguishable from the trees, flowers and waterways into which she blends.

The Lost Riverine Women also dress to blur into the land. The value of raiment as camouflage is a lesson we all brought with us from our lives before the Waterfall.

Ornamentation is just as strong, just as much of a shield. Marcasite's jeweled barrette never fades, whatever greenish-tealish wrap she craves, the barrette is sparkling clear. Sanadora effects small icons of her Healer Gods strung on her neck, her appendages, in her hair. Veronica Haze clings to the same kind of jewelry, but they are snatched by her demons, making her chase them to get them back, only to lose them again. Mirea, like Marcasite and her barrette, wears her wedding ring large enough to enwrap all of her.

I wear a ring that Jenny gave me, a circle of pearls around a clear turquoise-colored crystal set in silver, she claims to have found it on the ground. After showing it to everyone she could see, none of whom claimed it, she brought it to me. It is a gorgeous stone, but its bright blue clarity leads to no portals, no visions, the pearls do not evoke the seas of my time, there is no connection to anyone or anything but the mystery of its origins. It is simply a beautiful piece of jewelry, just another enigma in this holy unholy world.

VERONICA HAZE

A trail leads down to the edge, because everyone likes the up-close experience. There is a platform, railed and posted with dire warnings to be careful, don't fall in the falls.

They are spectacular, these marquis falls. Front page of the brochure, these falls. Ansel Adams was here, these falls. They want to be seen close up, they want to be *appreciated*.

There, her name was Veronica. Here, her name is Haze. When she approached this waterfall, it was with a grace and acceptance that she believed would carry her to a better world. Like all suicides, she was wrong - beautiful, mystical as it is, this is not that better world they are seeking.

Veronica Haze's demon was the voice in her head, ever-present, constant but changeable, telling her stories about other worlds. Dangling carrots of better places, better lives, where her special gifts would be revered. Taking over her dreams, asleep and awake, as the voice infiltrated her brain. Plumbing her subconscious for her deepest scars, offering the comfort that she craved in exchange for her trust. Becoming multiple voices to frame her personal, internal mythology. *Trust the voices - they come from Above.*

But a spinning voice does not shape reality. Believing in the truth of her vivid, abstract dreams, spending her time in deep trance states with her voices and visions unleashed in their full-throttle glory does not alter waking reality. She judged the world around her by her visions, applied her own visionary standards to other people, and everyone came up lacking. Feeling less and less at home in the world, she craved a home that did not exist, built in her imagination by the voices. As her belief in the voice grew, she made more and more decisions based on what they said. Decisions that worked out remarkably well at first, increasing her trust in them and following them deeper into madness. The stories the voices told her grew more outlandish, and she believed. The carrots grew more enticing. Her delusions of special gifts blossomed and spread. She grew more detached from more people who no longer understood her, as she no longer understood them, rejected more and more of the world. She became more and more isolated, more dependent on the voices for comfort, companionship and direction. Her actions and decisions became more bizarre and the effects were very detrimental. More and more, she was forced to face the evidence of her poor decisions, evidence of the poor guidance from the voices. The more her world shattered, the more lost she became, but the voices were the only thing she trusted for answers. In her shattering, she could no longer separate rationality from the carrots dangled by the voices. Her isolation was complete, she tottered on the brink of homelessness and the only available help was from the voices.

Shut away, she descends deep into the voices, tastes the promises of better worlds. All that she is shown, all that she has been shown over the years that she has heard them, brings her to conclude that there is no more value in this world, no place for her here. No good reason to stay. There are portals, she knows where to find them.

On her last day, she is at the famous waterfall, a two-day journey on the last of her meager funds. This waterfall has been calling to her for some time now, by way of the voices. A gateway to those other worlds she is now ready to claim and explore. She has always been drawn to water, it is fitting. She has turned away from so much in favor of the voices in her head that to her, this world is nothing more than shallow sand. There is no kind of foothold for her in this world.

Such beauty, this waterfall. The delusions of her private worlds have blinded her to the beauty of the real world and destroyed any desire to seek it out. But here, now, *this*. It is as if whatever holiness is to be found in this world has gathered and encapsulated in this one breathtaking place, this beautiful portal.

How can a place like this exist in such a disappointing world? How could such a place not be a portal to the divine worlds she has seen? All of the imaginary faces she gave to the voice come alive here, now, given form in her sight by the power of this raging, dazzling place. Smiling, welcoming, assuring her that they will be there, for her, in these heavenly worlds.

The waterfall, wide and furious, speaks freely and she is astonished to recognize it as the voice she knows so well. There are only a few other people on the observation platform, so she waits, standing still and serene at the rail. Her face and skin tingle, coated with mist, caressed by the lacy foamy fingers of the waterfall. She feels the speed and power of the river careening over the edge, and her heart beats with the rushing water pounding downward. The smell of the falls in her nostrils, wet and electric, beads of mist coating her nose hairs. They want to be seen close up, they want to *embrace envelope enclose*, these falls. It's all here for her, through this door, all her dreams and visions, the home she so craves. The waterfall, an open edge, a ropeline to promised lands, spreads itself out as pure white mist, clings to her eyelashes and washes the corruption from her sight. The voice, it's strong in this waterfall, inviting her in. *This is the way to go home.* Down below, the mist takes shape in spirals and whorls, eyes and mouths form and morph snowflake-like, spidery clouds ready to part for her, waving hands eager to welcome her. The draw is seductive, she feels the pull of the falls, its cool fingers urge her in but she is not alone on the platform. She waits, she stands, still and strong, listens to the invitation, silently accepts.

And when she is alone, she jumps.

And when she emerges on this side of the Waterfall, it is without the voices that so filled her life. She kept the memories of promises and visions, everything the voices told her, everything they showed her, but those places, those things are not here, and she is confused. Haze. Here, her demon is the absence of the voices in her head.

Instead of trying to swat her demon and drive it away, she's trying to catch it. It buzzes around her, tiny but undeniable, in bold, twisty patterns. Frantic, she grabs, lunges, chases, but it eludes her. She tires herself out, collapses on the bank and pulls her haze around herself like a blanket until she has gathered enough energy to chase it again.

However fanciful, her fantasies were element-based, because that's all she knew. Despite her visions, she could only envision in elements that she knew from her material world. However fanciful, what grows in your head will always grow from the known and familiar, it's the limits of human capacity. Veronica Haze invested so much in the truth of what she thought she knew about mysticism, that there was no capacity left to comprehend the diselemental. She committed an act of displacement for the sake of relocation and is not only addled, but brutally stubborn in her unawareness.

HAZE STORIES

Veronica's haze is an angry place. She trails the enraged scent of wildfire smoke, cloying and yellow-brownish. The demon that buzzed so loud in her head, before, now buzzes silent, just out of reach. So much anger for something so easily dissolved. She clings to her belief that her portal remains open, that it exists in this world and she is entitled to free passage. She wanders, she tries to climb the falls, followed and led by her silent demon, in search of the unfindable. Angry that her real life was so lacking, that so much was promised, revealed, *prophesied*, and all of it was lacking. Angry that all she finds here tells her *this is it*, this is where she is and this is where she will always be. No other portals, no better worlds, none of the gods with whom she cavorted in her meditation visions. The worlds she frequented in her head are lost to her here, even in her head, as if she has been stripped of all capacity for imagination despite her memory of things she thought she was promised.

Here, *portal* means *loop* and *haze* means *blind. Blind* means *fragmented.*

When she is not wandering, she sits on the shore and reaches. If she reaches hard enough, she will grasp something. Reaches for the memories she knows she has, but can't escape to, reaches for recognition of a voice she will never hear. Her demon reaches back to her, but stays out of reach, laughs when she reaches too far and falls into the water, to be set upon by arachnids.

I believe she sees the Boatman, but she is coy about it. She is curious and afraid at the same time, distrustful of what she thinks she sees. Whenever she gets closer to curiosity than fear, her demon distracts her with its tortuous silence and she digresses.

There, she was a secret society of one. An occult priestess with the fading context of an outer world. Here, there is only her outer world and she disdains the size of it. The lack of scope. The limitations and the broken promises. Her so-called psychic gifts are powerless here, and therein lies the anger of her haze.

THE WATERFALL SPEAKS

I t is interesting to me how many waterfalls are called Bridal
Veil. It is not hard to see the association, it simply surprises me
that it is so easily applied. What does that say about the world
these waterfall girls left behind? And about the ones who came here
through falls called **bridal veil?**

Nereid knows more about hunger and craving than I do. **Bridal
veil** does imply a certain craving.

Craving. Rich as I am with witness to so many suicides, I am left
with only helplessness. They come to me, they sacrifice their lives on
my jittery edge. They try to leave their baggage on my shore and
purify themselves on my rocks, like human laundry. They crave such
desperate things; their baggage reeks of heartbreak. And I am the
antidote to none of it, with no power to stop them.

There are wide, vast lakes in this world, which Nereid loves to
swim. Whether or not she sees him, the Boatman trails behind. He
watches out for her, more than she sees and despite his other duties, he
always has an eye on her. For the dead never stop dying. They require
passage to their underworlds, by way of the Boatman, but once they
are dead, the timetable is his. The dead have no other way to measure
time but before death, after death, and before the Boatman comes.

Beneath the surface of these large waters are smaller worlds, open
yet contained. They are separate, and they overlap. Eels abound.
Arachnids. Other swimming things; they are not quite like fish, but

fish is the only known word. Some swim with fins, some swim with wings. Waterbabies, elusive, no two alike. Winged creatures - wings work just as well in water as in air. One has a humanlike torso and frog legs, another is a bundle of floating pink strands. If you can look at that one long enough, it might let you see how its strands form changing faces. One can only be described as moth-ish, but not really **moth**-ish, bright red-orange wings that can reach, and stretch, and grab. One is easily mistaken for the underwater greenery rich on the lakebottoms, he moves quickly and has many cousins, all very hard to see. One is globular, hairy, scraggly tufts trailing dreamily around his whale-like fins. The frog-legged one, who skirts the rocky wooded shores both under and above the water, it enjoys the adoration of minions of tinier things, and it can be capricious in its bidding. Despite the wide differences in their manifestations, they are all related in one way or another, they are all winged. They all belong to me.

Nereid feels the absence of the things which used to tempt her. The ships, boats, the Ishmaels and other sailors of her ancient world, they are absent here. She must keep her harassment to those who cannot be harassed. Those who live in and ply these waters hold no treasures, no offerings and no fear, because here there are no Gods. Only riddles, koans and conundrums.

But here, the sound of my voice is always heard. My roar cannot be erased by expanse, distance or denial. Fed by my own veins, these waters look still, but they too have their own flex.

Down there, under my skin, there are the same cat-and-mouse games that pass for survival in some worlds but here, there is no need to eat, no appetite for any kid of flesh. Here, it's about sharpening, the momentary thrill of winning a game that is not a game, for which there are no rules, because the objective does not translate here.

On the edges of these lakes, tucked away in shady coves, are other smaller waterfalls, more of my own fingers stroking, massaging the drift of this water world. Fed by my own veins. These edges, whether or not they masquerade as other portals, they call to Nereid, she who is so preternaturally, so dangerously curious. She walks on expert feet, swims on expert fins and she has no fear, but she will always find herself confined to this world. What looks, even feels like a portal she can enter will always be nothing more than an appealing and *colorful loop back to the water she thought she just left. She is still learning that **portal** is not the same as **secret**.*

Certainly, a waterfall has secrets, it could be said that a waterfall is nothing but a veil of secrets. These border cascades who bleed into each other, again, just my own fingers folding and unfolding, they beckon like every waterfall and Nereid can only answer. Each of my fingers spills into the same endless abyss, or to Nereid, just another deep dead end. But even these wide lakes bleed into the same central waterfall that is the heart of me, the portal that admits from only one side. Nereid feels her boundaries most strongly beneath this one. In the smaller falls, she skips up and down like a salmon, flits like a flat rock from lake to lake, leaves her tailfin footprints across meadow grass and canyon walls as well as waterskins.

Some want a wider gate than others. Some crave the big-love embrace from life, that large fierce love and protection of a Mother Bear filling and enveloping them, cushioning them from the hazards of living. In their eyes, why should not their weapon of suicide do the same? But a waterfall is not a cushion, it does not embrace.

*Here, **embrace** means **stimulate. Feed.***

So they choose a wider, softer-sounding portal. Only to find themselves here, in the same place as others who were not deterred by the erratic lack of containment of other waterfalls. Only to find that there is no more Mother Bear here than there.

*They are misguided from the start. A waterfall does not **embrace**.*

*And it was not my decision to be a bridge to their next world. They come close at their own risk, intent or not. I am no more siren than legend. Back away from the edge, from the rail, from the boundary, and view me from afar: no, farther: can you embrace **me** now? Are you wide enough now to embrace me? Can you back up even more, farther, higher, a birds-eye view? Can you contain me now?*

It was not my choice to receive sacrifice. I am no more God than vessel. Whatever embrace I have, I save for the victims of sacrifice, those thrown into my maw against their will. The Boatman is quick to receive, for loving transmission to a much different world than the ones who come in by suicide. Yes, Nereid's speculation is partly correct. Beyond that, she is incapable of envisioning all that such other worlds might be, limited by her death and confinement here. And I am no more God in those worlds than I am in this one.

HIDDEN GODS

Who walks beside you when you're dead? Here, there, or anywhere?

Jenny says, ghost stories older than the Waterfall walk among us.

We want to control who walks with us in life and death but when it comes to the ineffable, it is no more controllable here than anywhere.

It's not just demons. Everyone here searches for their Gods, believing at first that they should be here. They are not here and some never accept that, never stop searching. Some mistake demons, eels, other winged things, even trees, rocks and rivers for their Gods. Some that can't find them, create them from the footsteps they think they feel beside them, behind them. We all seek an edge in uncertain worlds, and I am far from omniscient but I know enough that these Gods they create will never be their own.

On occasion, I too feel something unexpressed beside me, behind me. See something unclear flit in and out of sight almost before I notice, a brief reflection in the water mirrors. Something hidden is there.

Here, I have lost all grasp of what gods are, what makes them gods, yet I know a God when I feel one.

I am not unfamiliar with Hidden Gods, they pass through

other worlds, too. Half there, half here for a moment, then gone. Their purposes, motivations unknowable. Unreachable.

These Hidden Gods, they represent that they cannot be defined, that they are without form. They say they are only known by what they are not, but this cannot be believed. The Boatman says, much like the waterbabies, these cryptic, cloaked Gods are old beyond age, spent, retreated into a dimension in which they can heal, regenerate, regrow. They will be there for an even longer time than they were Gods, before they can be Gods again.

Is this to be believed? Hmm. I ask, *Why do I see them here?*

He shrugs. Either he doesn't know, doesn't want to tell, or hasn't invented that part yet.

So is there no One here to guide us, to be the God each one of us so desperately needs? No One to pray to, no God of All Gods to worship and implore?

He does not acknowledge the question.

From my time, I know better than to wish for the patronage of any one God. Divine patronage always comes at a price. But need sometimes makes that price worth paying and here, there is powerful need. Even I am not immune.

In my trickster days, when I was sentenced by Poseidon to accompany the victims of my follies to Hades' shore, it could be said that I rode that boat more times than anyone but the Boatman himself. Holding the dead in my arms, I felt the pale and diluted colors of loss reaching through vibrations of dissipating flesh, fighting to keep hold. They took parts of me with them, I took parts of them with me, and I saw the parts they left behind with grieving loved ones who cling to what is truly dead.

they have so much time to be dead

Their loved ones will not resurrect them, with their possessive hearts. Some veils will not be repaired, others will never be torn, not by the hands of the living or the dead.

At the end of those long and painful journeys, I was battered, often in body, always in spirit. Once in a while, I was met by Persephone, a shadowy Goddess even in her own realm, who plucked me from the Boatman to stroke my brow and feed me tea in her dark-jeweled lair. As the daughter of an exacting and powerful Goddess, she shared a certain sympathy with my plight. Where Poseidon and my victims heaped guilt upon my disgraced head, she was content to let me cry, to pour my guilt out into her dark rivers, to let it be washed away like a baptism. When I was spent, and the shaking had subsided, she returned me to the Boatman, still waiting on her shore.

Because I loved her, sometimes I wish it is her that I see in that fleeting reflection, that silent footstep, but that would mean she is spent, no longer the Goddess she once was. Nonetheless, I wish for her here, for something like her to put the last seal of divinity on this locked-away world and give me some kind of rudder by which to steer. To be someone who did not come here by waterfall suicide, who was here first, before me. Someone who heals rather than punishes, opens rather than conceals. Whose very name is a prayer and a promise of redemption.

Some here join cults of Gods created by others such as Rohini and Suzette's Blue Star cult, after Rohini's lost infant daughter. Some stay longer than others - as long as they draw something of what they crave from this false God, they stay; when realization sets in that what they crave is not there, they move on. Some to other cults, some to solitary and confused wandering, searching. Some, to bruised and confused solitude.

Those who have created their own Gods have stayed with them, too stubborn or impervious to see beyond their wishful creations. Rohini, with the cult devoted to her infant daughter, needs no more than to devote herself to the idea of a daughter she was not allowed to have. Coming from a world where daily life and tradition were bound to ritual, she has created an elaborate system of ceremony and sanctity in honor of her Daughter Goddess. Suzette has remained by her side, for reasons I cannot see.

Rohini has staked out a wooded grove for her shrine, in which she has built an idol of her Blue Star, an elaborate, idealized baby figure with a child's pudgy body and incongruous, all-knowing eyes that are not alive but can only be described as *alive*. It is incredible, brightly painted and jeweled, and I wonder where she got the materials. She has surrounded it with piles of flowers and glittering stones and I am amazed that the flowers allowed themselves to be cut. Perhaps the sheer power of her devotion overcomes their possessiveness, or maybe they feel her grief and feel sorry for her.

It inspires me to build a shrine to Persephone, a God I did not create, but whose presence in my existence is acutely missed. Far away from the others, I search until I find a cave which burrows deep under the water, then comes out in a dripping underwater chamber after a long, dark swim. The stalactites and stalagmites in this cave are unparalleled, worthy of an Underworld Goddess. The chamber is lit by a subdued, unspoken source, an uneven and changeable light playing like a slow borealis up and down the element-like formations and their roots. The underground aquifer spills down the spired wall, a thin sheet washing over the gothic formations. Streaks of yellow-orange, mineral green, silver and blue glow wet under the clear water veil.

Deep in this abysmal cave, I can still hear the Waterfall over the underground echoes of burbling stream and the light hiss of the falling watersheet. A most fitting shrine. I spend much time there, sitting alone on the edge of the water, praying to Persephone, praying that she find some way to make her comforting presence known here in this locked-away otherworld. Praying that she finds some way to tell my mother that I love her. I have brought several small stones, who agreed to accompany me, knowing that if they do not like it here, they will be gone. On the other side of the subterranean pond, there is a large stalagmite that is vaguely woman-shaped, surrounded by a nearly perfect circle of smaller formations. The more I sit and contemplate her, the more my eyesight bends to the face and figure of a woman, a woman who is beginning to look familiar. I swim across the water and place my glittering stones around her base, swim back to the other side and view the result. The stones are still there! Will they remain?

The pillar itself now shows signs of inner life. The seams and veins of the mineral formations glow with faint streaks of pink, green light, morphing to blue, maroon light, into violet, silver light. It shines, it glows, and I wonder if mine are the only eyes that can see it. It is entrancing, enchanting, like a bit of Persephone's world bleeding through to this one. The pillar takes on an even more womanlike shape, but despite the wonderous transfiguration, I hold no delusions that this has anything at all to do with the real Persephone. She is merely my wishful illusion.

No matter. Illusions hold their own comfort. I will make this Her shrine, regardless of Her absence and it will be my secret sanctuary - with no illusions that it really is *secret*.

I remain in my adytum for an unmeasured time - meditating, contemplating, sleeping, unbothered by anyone, anything. Even the eels are absent, and it cannot be because they don't know I am here. Before leaving, I swim back across and leave the pearl and crystal ring with the glittering stones.

Sometime later, I return to my hideout, watching to ensure I am not visibly followed, knowing that unseeable eyes follow me anyway. No one, not even the Boatman, has given any sign that they know about this place. When I arrive, the Goddess-shaped pillar is several inches taller, otherwise not much changed, but the sparkly stones I brought have multiplied and there are flowers growing around the base. The ring is gone.

The flowers, unlike anything I have seen growing here before, are similar to passifloras but the petals are multi-layered and multi-colored. They have not been placed here by someone else; they are growing from the stone floor of the cave.

It might not be a God of my invention or choosing, but something occult has settled here. A Goddess shines, but only in my own sight, only because I look?

HERE, REAPER

Helena's Goddess wears no flesh, bleached white skullbones draped in back-veiled robes, bony hands and feet barely visible at the floating edges. Hers is a very stern Goddess, not to be approached lightly. Not the happy, loving Mother Goddess of the pagans. Helena does not look to her for love, she looks to her for death.

Some are born with their eye on death. For them, all things romantic lead to death, cry out for death, bask in death. The dreamery of escape from their messed-up world. The fascination of the unknowable that is death. The lure of the dark. Some ritualize their fascination, adopt the vestments of death as their shield, offer up their living flesh on midnight altars and chase legends of jewel-lit afterlives. Helena's life was marred by losses of loved ones at a too-young age: first, her beloved grandmother at age seven, then the loss of her best friend and cousin to a heinous murder just one month later. Her grandmother was not an old woman, not infirm or ill, and it severely shook her seven-year-old understanding of death - that it took people who were old or sick. She was fed the usual platitudes of *gone to a better place, watching over us from eternity, angel wings* and so on. God loved them so much, he just had to bring them home early. This was affirmed when her best friend/cousin was killed – the good die young.

She bought the part about a better place. By age seven, she was already starting to understand the darker ways of her world. The thought of them watching her from above was creepy, and made her self-conscious and critical of everything she did. And what did that say about her - God didn't love her enough to take her to a better place? He left her here, because he loved them more?

The older she got, the more she felt abandoned by the God of her upbringing. Left behind to face this miserable world while others escaped to that so-called treasury of everlasting joy, it's not fair. The dangers of the world were all around her and the more attention she paid, the more people she noticed who died young. And unlike her beloved grandmother and best friend/cousin, some of these people didn't strike her as the kind that God would love so much that he had to have them home early. *How does that work?*

How does it really work?

The dangers all around her, it all leads to death. She sought, collected stories about young deaths: accidents, murders, illnesses, suicides. She ached to know how it felt to know you were about to die. How did it feel *not* to know - just *boom,* you're dead, no warning, no preparation? What it felt like to die. To be dead. To wake up dead on the other side.

To be the instrument, the decider of your own death.

She learned the stigmas attached to suicide, as she became more fascinated by it. She noticed that media stories about suicides were brief, with as little emphasis as possible on the act of suicide, and virtually no information about *why.*

And what of this *other side?* She rejected church images of God's heavenly kingdom as boring and absurd. *Then what?* Everything but harps and clouds and angels. If there's no angels, there's no devils, and that took away the fear of death and sparked her obsession with the mystery of what really happens.

maybe we go here... there... maybe we don't go anywhere....

She first attempts suicide at age fourteen. It is deemed a cry for help and she is treated accordingly. Angry and confused by her failure, she resists help and treatment and continues her obsession. She remembers a dream she had while unconscious from loss of blood, of a black robed woman with no face. Yet she saw a face, of sorts, bony and wizened, cold empty eye sockets agleam with a different kind of life - agleam with *death*. The woman said nothing, she simply lifted a skeletal hand as if holding an invisible bowl. Such wisdom Helena saw in those empty eyes, that fleshless face, in her anemic coma. Wisdom that could unlock eternity.

Helena does not reveal this image to her therapists but soon finds it in folkloric images and figures. She is seized - *She exists!* And She is Death.

She embraces her Goddess and cultivates a deathly appearance, surrounds herself with images and statuary. *Find me, take me home, here I am. Ready.* With the dangers of the world all around her, could her own death be far from hand? She does reckless things, takes unwise chances, to feel closer to death. Tempting death, teasing it, daring it to take her. *Here I am. Find me.* Welcoming the possibility with each careless risk. *Take me.* Envying those who make it. Fantasizing about the many, many ways to die. Picking and choosing the ways she finds most appealing, planning elaborate accidents. Imagining ways to attract her own murderer. Writing flowery letters to her Death Goddess, begging to be taken.

Her caregivers become alarmed. The offending wardrobe, makeup and tchotchkes are confiscated and disposed of. Her things are searched and her writings, books, suicide story collection, anything that can be related to her obsession with death are confiscated, analyzed and destroyed.

Outraged, she again attempts suicide and again fails. At the same time, the man who murdered her best friend and cousin is executed, a highly emotional event for her family on top of her repeat suicide attempt. She is bombarded with guilt - with the murder of their little one brought back fresh because of the execution, everyone around her was raw and no one was thinking straight. How did she think they would feel if they lost her, too, on top of this ongoing horror?

While she is thinking about that, she thinks about the execution of her best friend's murderer. He killed her, and for that he is rewarded with death? This is the most confusing thing she has ever heard. It wasn't God who sent her friend to a better place, it was him. The murderer. And it wasn't God who took the murderer to a better place, it was executioners. People choosing each other's deaths.

After she is released from the hospital, she is sent to a wilderness camp for troubled teens, where she meets more people who share her obsession with death and her contempt for their world.

Of course, there is a waterfall.

Deep in the wilderness, at the end of a grueling two-day hike, is a waterfall few get to see. A waterfall too beautiful to describe, tall and powerful yet much wider than it is tall. She is struck by the majesty of it, as if she is seeing something truly beautiful for the very first time, and she is surprised by her reaction to it.

In this waterfall, she sees waterfalls within waterfalls - split streams separate and tumble between rocky outcroppings, narrow offshoots go their own ways, tiny dainty streams ooze from the porous cliff rock, independent of the riverflow falling around them.

She feels the cool of the mist on her skin, in her hair, sees how the falling water loses itself and becomes mist, how the less powerful streams turn to low vapor and bounce off the bigger clumps of mist below them, never actually hitting the water down below, or the ground over which it floats. She is profoundly moved, as by nothing else in her life.

They set up camp downstream, where the waterfall can be heard but not seen. They will be here for days, focusing on clearing their cravings for self-destruction and other anti-social behavior by connecting with nature. Instead, she connects with another troubled teen, a boy named Trent who shares her obsession with death. Together, they sit by the waterfall, share their obsession, their thirst for death, their suicide attempts. She tells him about her skull-face Goddess, he shows her his oversize grim reaper tattoo. She sees beauty in the waterfall, with its dozens of offshoots, he sees a portal to death.

The waterfall as Death. *Of course!* She drinks in the beauty and contemplates this idea, the waterfall as death. In the little waterfalls within the waterfall, she now sees death within death. So many ways to achieve her ultimate desire. In the guided group meditations they are required to submit to, she closes her eyes, lays back and submits long enough to reach a trance state, then leaves the path of the guided journey and finds her way back to the waterfall, where she conjures the face and figure of her skeletal Goddess, whose dark black robes and trailing black veil float and flow with the falling water.

Death within death. Such power can only lead to death, which leads to...? She almost died twice. She could die again anytime, and not just by her own hand. *What if reincarnation is real? Then you just keep dying, again and again and again. What does it take, how dead do you have to be before you don't come back anymore? Before you stay dead, wherever death takes you?*

Ever since the death of her best friend and cousin, she has awoken every day wondering if it will be her last. Twice, she was certain it was. She and Trent sneak away from camp late at night, hike up to the top of the falls with a full moon. She shares her questions about death, reincarnation and more death; he is focused on the waterfall as suicide weapon.

Wouldn't they be screwed if we killed ourselves right here? Wouldn't they **all** *be so screwed?* he says, eyes wide with fire in the full moon light. He is nervous, pacing, back and forth and to the water's edge, then back and forth again.

They would indeed, she agrees. His outrage is contagious, fuels her own outrage at a lifetime of misery that brought her here, at the extreme violation - the rape of her privacy - that brought her here.

What are we staying here for, he says, arms waving, his back to the waterfall. *This bullshit nature experience? Let's shove this bullshit nature experience up their asses!* He reaches one arm toward the waterfall, roaring deathly downward, reaches his other hand out to her.

She stares, mouth open, thinks quickly. *What am I staying for? More of the same for a miserable lifetime?* She steps into a moment of comradeship, takes his hand and together, they jump.

Here I am, find me, take me home.

In the short moment of consciousness before she hits the water, her mind floods with all of the questions, all of the images, all of the ideas of death she has ever had. The adrenaline rush she has craved overcomes the instant of pain as she is demolished, body and bone, in the downpour.

His body is found in the morning, caught in the rocks of the campsite shore. Hers does not surface for three more days. When she gets here, she is alone, much to her surprise and even my own. They went in together - where did he go?

Another question that will never be answered.

CHATTER

There was no question that Helena's death was suicide. She and her companion in death were vocal malcontents at their wilderness camp, both were open and proud of their obsession with death, their failed attempts and how they would be sure to do it right next time.

Naturally, it was a huge scandal for the camp and its organization. Two at-risk youths with known suicidal tendencies killed themselves on their watch, exactly counter to the camp's advertised purpose. At first, camp officials tried to pass it off as an accident, but that was quickly debunked. The remaining troubled teens were whisked back to civilization, for fear of copycats, and the organization suspended operations, ran for shelter and braced for the lawsuits.

Back home, they knew she would never stay. Her family wallowed in guilt and blame, recounted her obsession with death and all the signs that led to her end, recast it all as post-traumatic stress from her early losses, blamed all they could point to publicly, blamed themselves privately.

Here, her name is Reaper. She is content with her suicide but not content *here*. She is disappointed that her Reaper Goddess is not here and has adopted her black-habit robes, but cannot achieve that skeletal visage. She wanders, searches, analyzes, still trying to figure out what this place is, what death really is. She gathers rocks and builds stone skeletons and the rocks amuse themselves by rearranging themselves into more abstract constructions. The fact that she lives and walks here means, to her, that she could die again, go to yet another place. The fact that her suicide mate is not here tells her there are indeed other places and her curiosity, far from being quenched by the waterfall, consumes her. While she is puzzled that he is not here, that there are only women here, she does not miss him, does not search for him. He was a kindred spirit, yes, but he was a temporary friend and she had no desire to spend eternity with him. Eternal togetherness was not why she jumped with him.

She wanders in her adopted black robes, which are heavy on her otherworld frame. Exhausted, she sits at the water's edge, stares at the Waterfall. To her, it still appears as the waterfall she went into, still shows her falls within falls, death within death. There must be ways to die here, she tells herself, ways to get to the next world. And the world after that.

She tries to climb up the waterfall so she can jump again, but she is still here. She has tried to drown herself and hang herself, but she does not breathe, so this does not kill her. She tries cutting herself, but she does not bleed. She has climbed to the high places and jumped, but merely floats unharmed to the ground.

She sees the Boatman, tries to swim to his boat to beg a ride to his other side, but he is crafty and stays out of reach. He does not explain why she sees him at all, why he teases her this way. Her demons wear the same black robes, taunt her with the skeletal hands and faces she cannot achieve. *So you think you know death,* they sneer, *you think you have really tasted death?*

But for her, one taste was not enough. It was too brief, too limited, this can't be all that is Death. This little waterfall world is not the only destination of death, that is proven by the absence of so many others. Many weapons, many deaths, many destinations? She searches out the boundaries of this world and hurls herself against them again and again, but they remain impenetrable. They do not expand for her the way they do for me. Here, as she did there, she prays for death, calls for her Reaper Goddess, begs for a fresh death and an end to this world, prays that each day here will be her last.

ENEMIES

Why *are there only women here?* As Helena Reaper demonstrates, men also commit suicide by waterfall.

There is no one to answer me. The Boatman laughs at my questions, points out that he is male.

Not the same. You did not commit suicide, you are not here by sentence, is my reply.

So often, a woman's worst enemy is herself. Women willingly submit to the demons that haunt them, feed and nurture the very torment that drives them down. Women drive themselves down with self-hatred bred from myriad sources, hate breeding contempt and more hatred. Is this why we're all women here, because no one can hate oneself like a woman?

Sometimes the search for God leads to suicide. The inability to connect with the Divine is its own burning hell - knowing others around you who bask in the ecstasy of their Gods, following so many promising paths, only to be rejected again, feeling that overwhelming desire to take shelter in the arms of the Divine, only to be denied. To be so beaten down as to feel that one's own God is the enemy.

To feel that one is a disappointment to God.

To embrace one's demons, one's enemies, in a gesture of defeat and surrender to the hell of disappointing one's God. To bury oneself so deep in this hole that one can never again believe in light.

When dark is so well known that light becomes the enemy, there is nowhere left to go but down.

And others are just as vulnerable to such enemies. They, too, seek waterfalls. So, why are there only women here?

NEREID

I am rich with witness.

As the first to come here, I have watched this world fill one by one as they arrived, with their stories and their baggage and their demons.

There was no one here to greet me, to pull me out of the water and orient me. When I arrived, this world was much smaller than it is now. I believe it expands, grows, with every new one that arrives.

When I arrived, I was very confused. I was clear that I had tried to commit suicide but unsure if I had succeeded. *What is this place?* At first, I thought my father or one of his enforcers had fished me out and he had found a new way to banish me. I remembered - still felt - the pain of my weakened half-nymph/half-God body ground and battered by the waterfall, but while in pain, my body looked intact. The scars of the breaking and shredding were visible, but my body, my flesh, felt profoundly different. *Am I dead?* And if so, had I truly, finally escaped Poseidon?

Time, if it can be so called, passed and I explored my new world, found no one else here but eels and other animalistic creatures. No nymphs, Gods, no humans. No one but me. This world as it was then was a vibrant green lush such as I had never seen. It has day but no sun, night with several moons.

And the moons do not limit themselves to day, nor do they always appear at night. Unlike the world from which I came, there are no predictable cycles. The Waterfall, framed with low-hanging rainbows, double rainbows with cloudy gray in between, triple rainbows with flickering lights in between, sends its mist all over the land and sometimes, mist is all the ground there is to walk on. The light, from its unknown source, is not as bright as sunlight, almost half-sun, half-cloud, not unlike the filtered light of an eclipse. Yet, things are sharper in this light, without the sunlight glare to obscure the finer, subtle details.

It was enchanting, and I felt peace — at the same time, I feared it was just another of Poseidon's prisons and at some point, I would be found and freed by Amphitrite. Returned to his world, back under his thumb.

More time, such as it was, passed and that did not happen. The memory pain of my waterfall leap slowly faded and I began to wonder if I really was dead. Wandering this world when it was smaller, I searched for clues and answers, but found none. I found rivers, trees, small lakes, plants and flowers, rocks and cliffs with faces, some with the ability (or the preference) to speak, but none willing to tell me anything. I found tiny snowmelt falls, miniature waterfalls like haiku, here one moment and gone the next. I found boundaries of my small new world and that inflamed my curiosity. I searched and prodded and tried to penetrate but found no chinks in the boundaries, no portals disguised or otherwise into or out of this world, other than the Waterfall.

I made the mistake of trying to climb back up the Waterfall to see where it went, only to be slapped down again and again and again before I decided it only opened one way. Since I have accepted that, I am able to climb to the top at will.

I got to know the nature of the eels, the winged things, saw my first waterbaby and spent much time trying to chase it, to get a better look, learn what it was. To find out if it had any answers for me. I watched over time as the visage of the Waterfall changed from the one that I went into, to the face it wears today.

More and more time passed without sign of Amphitrite, or anything to do with Poseidon. For all the water here, there is no ocean. Some of the lakes grew bigger, two or three became quite vast, but they are not oceans.

It was some time before I saw the Boatman. It was a joyful reunion, but I thought it meant my imprisonment was being relaxed and I would again be hauled before Poseidon.

Not so, said the Boatman. *Your suicide was complete.*

I am dead!

What is this place?

He cannot reach you here, was all the answer he would give. He did not explain why I was isolated here, why I had not ridden in his large boat to Hades' shore, or that later, there would be others. He said it took some time for him to find me. I was flattered that he would look. I did not have to ask for his pledge to keep my location concealed from my father, I believed him when he said Poseidon couldn't reach me here. He stayed for a while then disappeared and after he was gone, this world was much larger. There was more water, more land to explore and the Waterfall looked much less like the one in which I died.

I was alone, but not lonely. Who can be lonely in such a glorious, poetic world, with so much water? I had the Waterfall, the other animate things to keep me company. Much time was spent sitting in the presence of the Waterfall, on the shore, swimming under the onrush, feeling the Waterfall on my skin, in my ears, vibrating in my veins. Hearing the voice of the Waterfall, learning to separate it from the roar of water eroding rock, water hitting water. It was not easy - the voice of the Waterfall speaks as element, not mass, and I had to learn to understand.

I am still learning to understand. If I ever had a wish to leave this place, like so many do, it would not be until I have reached a fluent and consensual grasp of this tongue. It would not be until I finally understood everything the waterfall will ever say.

As the Waterfall is eternal, I expect to spend eternity deciphering it.

. . .

It was some time longer before the second one came through the Waterfall. I was as shocked at her arrival as she was. For days, the Waterfall had been behaving strangely - its voice had taken on a higher pitch, there was more mist than usual and the eels in the immediate area were agitated. I was thrust into what felt like a dream state, yet I knew I was not asleep. By then I had learned the difference between asleep and awake, as they are defined here and I knew this was different.

In this state, I could see her, standing ramrod straight on the edge of another waterfall, poised to jump. Gathering herself. The Waterfall in front of me began to shift, bulging and distorted, contracting and expanding as if heaving for breath. When it cleared, it was the waterfall on which she stood. The portal was open, and I was frozen with awe at the sight.

All at once, I could see her life, I could read her head. A woman old enough to have grown children, whose voices I could hear among the shouts and screams of the tribe advancing on her as she stood and readied herself to jump. Accused of a crime she did not commit, involving the death of a child of the leader of her people, she was being pursued to be executed in front of her people. Innocent, she chose to die in the dignity of the waterfall rather than endure the humiliation of public condemnation and execution, to preserve and deliver herself to an understanding God.

She stepped into a moment of acquittal and was delivered into my world. After I helped her out of the water, she lay on the shore, ragged and exhausted for three or four days. Her name was Theodite and as far as I know, her name remains Theodite. It was not until later that their names changed on coming here. As she became oriented to her new world, she looked to me to validate her innocence in the way of a judge, but I could not help her with that.

It was not enough for her. She accused me of obstructing her and went off alone. I did not see her or hear of her again until I found the Lost Riverine Women and saw her among them.

They came more frequently after Theodite. Each with a story, a reason. Each with a reaction to this world that differed from mine, and from each other's. Each trying to escape something, because after all else has been stripped away from their reasons for suicide, that is the only reason to destroy oneself: to escape.

But each of them was human. I was not. Had I not committed suicide, would I still be alive in my old world, still roaming the seas and waterways, still playing devil for my amusement and running from an angry God?

I am happy and unhappy here, restless and content. Or maybe those four elements balance me into a kind of neutrality - here, *neutral* means *rooted, cozy*. I feel everything and I feel nothing. And I have long ago stopped looking over my shoulder for the long arm of my father's law.

PRETTY

Her first addiction was to her own beauty. The intoxication of it was spoon-fed to her by her mama and her grandmama, and reinforced by her daddy and the standards of his world. *Such a pretty little girl.* And such things her beauty would buy: all she would ever need, it traded on her beauty. *Such a pretty girl, she'll want for nothing.*

Her mama pushed hard, as she had been pushed by her own mother. She learned all about enhancements, about the need for them, all the necessary beauty skills. Being pretty is very hard work and the work is never done. Her mama was pretty but not pretty enough, despite her advanced skills, and she needed her daughter to be as pretty as she herself should have been. Prettier. There were greater heights to be reached than what her mama had obtained, and more than anything, her mama wanted those heights for her pretty, pretty daughter, whose glory would reflect on her. Makeup, hair, clothes, maintenance, skill. It was assumed there was no other path for her and she was groomed accordingly.

And she loved it. She thrived on it: the attention, the praise, the narcissism. But like her mama, she wasn't pretty *enough.* Words like *beautiful, stunning, gorgeous, breathtaking,* were not applied to her. Her mama and grandmamma knew it, and they pushed her harder. There was always more she could do, more to achieve; she could never relax, never say *here I am, at my best* because someone else was always prettier. She had to compete. She had to be more than pretty, she had to be a ravishing beauty.

Her mama pushed her into the cutthroat world of beauty pageants, but others were prettier and no matter how well she was enhanced, she couldn't compete. And no amount of pushing by her mama was going to change that. Her prettiness - by the standards of her world - peaked in adolescence, and she was the first to see it. It stared back at her in the mirror, that first look at her grown-up face, at the woman she would soon be, and it was not as pretty as it was yesterday. On that day, she knew she would never be pretty enough, she would never be *beautiful*, and she didn't know what to do.

What did you expect, said her mama, *did you think you were **it**?* It was a direct contradiction of what she had always been told, and she was shocked and confused. From her mother, venom where there had always been support? She had heard her mama spit venom before, but not at her. Never so hurtful. *Oh now, she's prettier than all those other girls*, said her daddy, unconvincing. The pageants stopped. If she couldn't win it all, her mama told her, that made her a loser. Why bother? She would have to learn to settle for the limitations of her prettiness. She might get a good husband, but not a *great* husband. Not the kind of big-money prize her mama had missed out on, the kind of catch her mama hoped she would be pretty enough to get. Her mama's disappointment was clear. There were plenty of things her mama hoped to gain by her marriage to a great (rich) man, at the same time, her mama blamed herself for not attracting a more handsome husband - beauty plus beauty breeds more beauty and clearly, she had failed at that.

In one day, she went from pretty and promising to genetic failure. She was thirteen.

So she discovered other enhancements. She might not be able to look prettier, but she could feel prettier. Her mama helped a little bit with that, too, keeping the house well-stocked with champagne and white wine – ladies' drinks, not really *drinking*, just feeling good; and more secretively, gin. It always helped Mama feel prettier than she really was. When Mama graduated to pills, so did she, easily helped by the open medicine cabinet and Mama's amply-stocked makeup table, nightstand, purse, kitchen drawer. Mama didn't care any more about counting her pills than she did about measuring her liquor bottles.

But Mama's chemical enhancements accelerated her aging skin and body and her addiction grew as her beauty fled. One day her mama woke up dead, in full makeup and her prettiest nighty, full of liquor and pills. It was ruled an accident, but she was not so sure. Her mama's beauty had long lost its buying power and without it, she was lost. Her mama died because if she wasn't pretty, she was nothing.

If she wasn't pretty, she was nothing.

She was bereft when her mama died. Without her mama to push her, would she know what to do? She needed to be pretty to get her through life, and she needed her mama to guide her on that. Her grandmama was already gone and her daddy was no help, lost in his own grief and unschooled in the ways of mentoring beauty. His guidance consisted of a higher allowance, a new car, and unlimited freedom with a see/hear no evil approach. It wasn't his fault, he didn't know what else to do. She was forced to size herself up, assess her prospects and figure out what she had to work with and make the most of it.

It required enhancements. Makeup, pills. Expensive hair, coke. The latest clothes, speed. Social charm, alcohol. Plastic surgery, narcotics. Daddy paid for a lot more than he knew. But others were prettier.

She lost sight of any long-term plan and became obsessed with *prettier*. The enhancements helped her forget, for a while, that her own mama had pronounced her a loser, never pretty enough. And it was never enough, no matter how enhanced, it would never be enough. Others would always be prettier. As hard as she worked, as much as she enhanced, she couldn't make herself as pretty as some others, but she could feel prettier.

Until she couldn't.

The waterfall was an impulse - she could easily have taken her mama's way out. Her daddy had dragged her off to rehab, but she didn't come out feeling any prettier. When a down-on-his-luck business associate of her daddy's prodded his son, her sort-of boyfriend, to propose to her, she was relieved. She said yes, and felt a little prettier.

But he treated her as if he had settled for less than he deserved, and she turned back to her chemical enhancements. She knew she had also settled, so she didn't blame him for feeling the same. With the enhancements, she felt a little prettier, but never enough. Like her mama, she got crafty with her secrets, maintaining just enough on the outside to hide most of it.

It wasn't planned, she had not been having conscious suicidal thoughts; nothing so conscious as a plan. It was a camping trip, something she enjoyed because she could always be prettier than anyone else in the wilderness. It's all a matter of priority packing.

And so very carefully packed were her pills, her flasks, her secret bottles. There was usually a lot of drinking on these camping trips, so she blended right in. And she was prettier than the other camper wives, or rather, she wore more makeup and paid more attention to her hair and clothes. On closer, boozier inspection, she was not really prettier. What is it about these women - hair carelessly skinned back in flippy little ponytails, make-up free faces glowing with the beauty of the nature that surrounds them, figures looking frumpy in unglamourous camping outfits - what is it about them that makes them prettier? They smiled, they laughed, they joked with their husbands, each other, and their faces overflowed with beauty. She felt like a painted-up freak.

She kept her alcohol level up, with easy-reach pills tucked into every pocket and crevice of her clothes and gear. They were camped in a gorgeous place and that made her feel worse - the wilderness was prettier. The trees, flowers, river, waterfall, all were prettier. She was nothing. The natural beauty all around them had an obvious effect on the others in her camping party, including her indifferent husband. They gazed around, eyes glazed with drink, waxed rhapsodic about the charms of their surroundings. *Such incredible beauty!*

How she ached to be so described. She looked around through her own glazed vision and wondered what it was about it all that was so enchanting. How can she compare herself to a tree? A river? How can she compete? She felt the loss of a world in which she had never gained any real footing, with no solid base to replace it. She had her husband - for now, until his indifference became intolerance and then absence and removal. What then? She wasn't getting any prettier.

The waterfall was an impulse. Close to their campsite, it was an easy gathering place. Everyone brought their flasks - they were partying! Plus, she had her pills. The tipsy conversation turned to the waterfall and soon they were competing with each other, each trying to outdo the others with their wordy worship of this beauteous waterfall.

She listened to them describe the waterfall in ways that should have been about her. She should have been the most beautiful thing they had ever seen, her mama told her so, her grandmama, her daddy used to tell her so. Furtively, another pill. She looks at the waterfall while they speak, tries to apply their words to what she sees. Such a pretty waterfall. Such beauty. Such power. Such worship.

The campfire turns to stories about waterfalls, urban mythology and crude folklore. Human sacrifices made to waterfalls. Suicides of the lovelorn in waterfalls. Tragedies caused by greedy waterfalls. She is attentive, silent. She pulls from her flask and covertly, another pill. The appearance of the waterfall softens as the stories grow more bloodthirsty. Greedy, beautiful waterfall.

On her last day, she wakes up in this place of natural splendor, thick verdant forest in green flower, misty-blue morning dawn. She has been dreaming of her mama, and the waterfall, in ways that are abstract and unremembered when she first awakens. Sitting around the morning campfire, sipping a cup of coffee that is far more brandy than it is coffee, with her morning pills, the sound of the waterfall pounds her aching head. Something in her dream about her mama, and this waterfall, bothers her. Everyone else in her camping party is nursing a similar hangover, minus the pills, and their morning talk rings in her ears, competes with the snap of the campfire and the roar of the waterfall.

Somebody says something innocuous, the fire crackles and something snaps in her head. Her mama, in the dream, comparing her to the waterfall. If only she was this pretty, her mama had said, then she'd really have something. Just like her mama used to say when she was drunk, comparing her to others.

But I'll never be that pretty. It hits her, right there, the full force of her failure to be pretty enough. *I'll never be that pretty.* Not even as pretty as these unenhanced women, laughing off their hangovers without even caring that they were so much prettier.

She takes another pill, no longer cares if anyone sees her do so. Without speaking, she refills her brandy cup, slips another pill and slips off from the group. It's an easy path to the waterfall.

How dare you, she says to the waterfall. *How dare you be prettier than me.* As soon as she has this thought, she knows how ridiculous it is. Another pill. *But they worship you. You are worshiped and adored like I should have been. But I pale before the sight of you as I pale before all who are prettier. As I pale before everyone.*

The waterfall is softer than last night, in this brilliant-hued morning light. Its roar is muted by the brandy and the pills, so that she hears her mama's voice coming back from the dream: *Never be pretty enough. I wasn't, you aren't, see? Witness the waterfall. Witness what it did to me. What it will do to you.*

More brandy and she slips into a moment of indifference, shocked wide awake by the cold water for one frigid, terrible moment, but soon *out,* unconscious on a rock. Drowned in the falls. Her mama's voice is drowned forever.

But she lives on here, the voice of the waterfall softer here, neutral. Devoid of her mama's voice. But her demons have followed and they will be the voices she thought she left behind. They come at her with huge, mascaraed eyes and lipstick sneers, fluttering elongated lashes and telling each other they are prettier than she is.

Here, her name is Pretty. No prior name matters; Pretty was all she ever wanted to be. And we are content to let her be the prettiest among us, that is an easy thing. But she still thinks the waterfall is prettier, that we are all prettier, that she will never be pretty enough.

PRETTY CHATTER, PRETTY STORIES

There is no competition here - nothing for which to compete. Pretty has her name, her title as it were, and it all belongs to her alone. She is the prettiest one here because she needs to be, and but for her demons, she is free to be at peace with it.

There, the competition was poisonous to body, mind and spirit. It wasn't so much that the ones who were prettiest won, it was more that the ones with the least flaws and sometimes, the best connections won. Everyone involved, from top to bottom and a wide periphery in between, was in the business of sniffing out flaws, examining, magnifying and dissecting them. Tally them up, judge them and score: *We have losers!*

The competitions tore her down and her mama built her back up again. Always a new beauty trick, another slight-of-hand. Until the day when there was no more keeping up, the day she was left too far behind to ever catch up. The day her mama withdrew her support, confirmed she was a loser.

Her mama: her first demon.

But for her demons.... Demons feed on that which drove us to suicide. With their exaggerated makeup-faces, they plague her with mirrors, slight-of-hand objects flicked a certain way to catch her unexpecting eye with distorted reflections. They chase her as she runs, shivering, to the water's edge, desperate for a prettier reflection. Sometimes she finds one. Sometimes she doesn't.

Often, it's just the face of an eel. But she doesn't know this, she is too destroyed to hear me say it. It is her own pretty face often enough for her to continue to seek it.

When she died, her indifferent husband was shocked and guilty, because he was drunk and didn't notice she had wandered away from him and the others. He was left with her devastated father, still grieving the loss of his wife, and endless reminders of her need to be pretty. He was burdened with the wrenching and impossible task of helping her prostrate father decide which photos to keep, what to put away where no one would ever look at it again, what to simply throw out. Although like her mama, her death was ruled an accident, her husband was not so sure and it bothered him a great deal. If people thought it was suicide, they would blame him. But shouldn't he be blamed? He feared it might be so. He paid for his indifference with a lifetime of guilt and insecurity, a lifetime of fear of her, her mama and her father, watching him from wherever they went when they died, judging him, condemning him for his indifference. His poor stewardship of that which he agreed to care for.

She had no friends among women. The three women who were part of her final camping party were not close friends, they were the partners of her husband's friends. One, she had never met before that weekend. They were horrified by her death and also felt guilty for not watching over her, but they didn't know her well enough to opine whether it was accident or suicide. Their husbands/boyfriends, who knew Pretty's husband fairly well, but not Pretty, discussed it among themselves and with their women. Most of what they knew about her, they heard from her husband and they were aware of his indifference. But suicide is an uncomfortable thing to witness, from any angle, and they felt a little better agreeing among themselves that it was just a horrible accident.

It was an accident, said her husband, *she would never kill herself.* No further explanation was needed.

But her father: her poor father. The double loss of his wife and daughter was too much for one man to take. They were both accidents, tragic accidents, but why them? Why him? It was a blow from which he never recovered and he withered into ill health that took him within a year of his daughter's death. Is that not another method of suicide?

As for Pretty, she sees that we are all here by suicide and wonders if her mama is here somewhere. But her mama did not exit by waterfall, she is not here. Sometimes she searches for her mama, but the effort is half-hearted at best. Part of her feels the relief from the pressure to be prettier, and doesn't want her mama to bring it back. At the same time, she was always a girl in need of her mama, and that was the only kind of mama she knew. There are motherly types here, willing to adopt ones in need, but it is rarely a healthy adoption. They do not interest Pretty because they don't care how pretty she is.

She is confused by the lack of men here. Men were her primary audience, what does she do without them? I don't know if she can see the Boatman - I have never seen them in each other's presence, which means nothing, and she has never mentioned him to me, which also means nothing.

By now, she has gathered enough of herself to see the folly of thinking she had to compete with a waterfall for a beauty title. If anything, she now looks to the Waterfall as her mama, because it was the Waterfall that washed away the pressure of *prettier.* She is not sure that is what she intended with her inebriated, spontaneous suicide and despite the relief of it, it will take her a long time to get used to it.

To her, the Waterfall is the only guidance she has. But it speaks a language she doesn't understand, it heightens senses she cannot grasp. The Waterfall is element, it speaks as element, and element is a difficult tongue in a diselemental world.

LEGENDS AND SPECTATORS

Any extraordinary phenomenon in nature is bound to attract legends. Is bound to inspire legends. Stupendous, gigantic waterfalls, famous for size, depth, power, beauty. The vain and the power-hungry seek to attach their names, their images to these falls. The unbalanced seek connection with God, or escape, or both. The users seek to harness all of it for profit. The rest just want to revel in the power, the blessing, of such splendor.

Such waterfalls draw constant lines of gawkers, an ever-present audience always too happy to see something extraordinary and unexpected happen. For those who seek an audience for what they do, here it is.

The Waterfall has grown rich with witness. In the beginning, the Waterfall knew only itself, as the world was smaller and less populated. Slowly, small spirits congregated at its waters, as well as in the surrounding trees, rocks, flowers, mountains, making it alive. When it broke into the world of humans, it instantly became legend. Surely this is a breach between worlds, thought the people, where the force of the Gods spills forth.

Legend has it that some who went into the falls were reborn as Gods

Legend has it that the Waterfall has a taste for sacrifice

According to legend, an unhappy girl went into the falls and flew out as a dove

According to legend, a crippled boy went into the falls and flew out as an eagle

Legend has it that people who feed an angry waterfall enjoy prosperous lives

victory over enemies

dominion over nature

infinitum.

And legends draw spectators. First the spirits, then the tribes. When tribal traditions waned, the spectators still came, tourism fueled by the majestic power of the falls and the potency of legend.

As time moved and times changed, legends grew around more recent events. Stunts. Accidents. Suicides.

Some crave witness of their final act. The waterfall itself is not enough witness, suicide letters are not enough witness. Loved ones, strangers, must see what they do because only if they witness, will they truly understand. And the waterfall will draw the witness they crave.

They know the legends, that's part of the draw. By their very public suicide, they hope to become part of the legend. The depth of their suffering is such that only maximum witness will do, and the yearning for legend is strong in some souls. I, Nereid, am not here to explain, but can only strive to understand and translate into digestible terms. Understanding is an act of its own.

But then they come here, where things are not so public. These ones who crave public sympathy and public embrace of their pain, they have no audience here. There is no *public* here.

No one here but each other, and me. Most others are too wrapped up in their own pain to notice the suffering of others. I have little sympathy, I only observe. But small groups form, most of which eventually dissolve. They clump together, hoping strength in numbers will overcome... something. Some come together over the fact that they all went down the same waterfall, believing that makes them the same. But they are not the same, and when they figure this out, they separate. Some

gravitate back to one another, still trying to overcome...
something.

They are not alike, but for the choice of their final act. Some
are so shy that they chose suicide as an antidote to the loneliness born of their shyness, and whose only public statement of
self was their very public suicide.

Here, they don't understand how such a large gesture
brought them to such a secluded place. Where everyone is
broken, against the backdrop of pure natural beauty that can
never be broken, that is our waterfall world.

A most prolific waterfall, these famous places that are only
one of thousands of outer faces of one Waterfall. There are
ones who chose to die in them hundreds, thousands of years
before the waterfalls became famous, they are all here. Their
reasons are much more basic than the ones who came here in
more modern times, and most of them shun each other, each
believing the others can't understand.

Are these threads supposed to weave together, into a
blanket of one suffering, one healing? Where is the needle, the
shuttle and loom, for a task that will never be complete?

A LIFETIME OF WATER

Born from a Water Spirit and a Water God, I had the sea in my veins. Sea water and fresh water are two different things and the worlds they cover and contain only overlap to a certain degree. I kept mostly to the sea because that is what best fit my feet, but I also knew fresh waters.

Oftentimes, I hung close to the shores, near the places where freshwater rivers empty into the sea. Where two worlds become one. The dominant force - the sea - swallows the rivers, but not before they flood the sea with an adulterating force and the debris they have managed to drag this far, as well as the water creatures which thrive in both waters. Swimming in it, I felt the lightness of the fresh water, always a different temperature than the sea rushing to absorb it. I smelled and tasted the land that it carved, the indigenous greenery, the inland creatures who called it home and the bodies it claimed. Strange and exotic, these silky sediments floated through my fingers and caught in my hair, settled around the seaweed or caught the ocean currents to erode into the sea. I heard the prayers made to the waters and the stories of those who worked and died in them, broken into smaller and smaller fragments the closer they got to the sea. I collected what I could for the fun of puzzling them back together on those solitary nights in the places I went to hide, or was held prisoner. The results were inconclusive, and the crazy-quilt collages they made resembled nothing close to their original intents. It didn't stop me from filling in the blanks myself and adopting what suited me. It's the treasure trove of the waters.

When the Almighty Sea God made the first waterfall, bursting over a high and mighty cliff into the sea, I was not there to witness its birth. But word spreads fast on water currents and soon I was there, floating offshore, witness to its infant stages.

The entire mountain exploded, spewing water instead of lava. The roaring, broiling outrush and the mist, the foam, the churning chaos down below, it was a phenomenon never before seen. What started as a single split cliff spilling forth one falling river had grown beyond monumental by the time I saw it. It was weeks, months this way, growing in height, breadth and power every day while I watched.

One day, the gargantuan waterfall shuddered and heaved, the sight of it blurred in a way I have since come to know well. The sea all around me quaked, and I was bounced out of range by the swells. When I returned, the waterfall had shrunk to its original size, still huge, but one river falling from one split cliff. But now, there were other waterfalls on other rivers large and small. The force of the waterfall, too much to be contained in one place, had turned itself inside-out, proliferated and spread.

Some fell on other seashores, those were my favorites. But the first one never lost its pull.

Such a draw that I was not always smart about it. It became a favorite rendezvous, and as such, it was easy for Poseidon to catch me there. And if not there, another seashore waterfall. First, I was banned from the seas, then from the fresh waters and my world was too small to be called a world. Under his ever-heavier thumb, I suffocated and shrank, until he believed me too small to be any more trouble. I slipped away and made my way back to the waterfall, the original waterfall, his water-fall. Here, I would make my stand, I would take two things that he made and make them one.

From a lifetime of water, I stepped into a moment of *water-*

fall, into a moment of weakness, intoxication and control. Cool and aery, it became me, like a wedding veil. It welcomed me, set aside its own devastating power to let me feel mine. Just as I have water fins and land feet, I have a God's life and a mortal's death. In my weakened state, I was as vulnerable as any human or animal and I knew this when I jumped. My intent was clear, with full knowledge that it was suicide, and my bones shattered and disintegrated like any human's. The waterfall, acting as portal and weapon for the first time, received me gently and drowned me quickly and when I awoke, broken and water-logged on the other side, the voice of the Waterfall was the first of my new awareness. The feel of the Waterfall was misty-soft on my new skin and the silvery taste of it was still in my mouth. The scent of it was the scent of all watery things and when my new vision cleared, adjusted to a new and different light, the Waterfall was there, the center point of my afterlife.

Here, I am done stirring things up just to see what will happen. There is no ability or capacity, and I have learned that it does not serve me. If I knew what served others, I would tell them, but here, my vision as it has so far developed, still only sees in fragments. Even my own picture is not clear.

here. To them, surrender is a one-step process and death is never-ending.

Light, dark, both can be never-ending if that is what you seek. I would be starved without both. And when they interplay, still more that is covert can emerge. All beauty is made of light and dark; without one the other is sterile, infertile. For what is **waterfall** but **water**, the root of all growth, the root of all sustenance and here, **sustenance** means **balance**. Light without dark, dark without light, is imbalance. Nothing is definable without the perimeters of its opposite. Nothing is famous without both. Nothing ends until the next beginning and nothing begins until something ends.

And there is no clean without dirt. Waterfall might wash you clean as you go in, but you come out bloody and muddy all over again.

They can stay asleep as long as they like, drying out on my shore; time and this world will wait for them. This world will embrace them whether or not they are willing and they will learn that rejection of one world does not translate to rejection of all worlds. They will learn that form is transitory and color is fleeting, that their moment in time was wasted. They will learn that distance is not measured by endurance and that time does not heal anything here. They will learn that the larger the pain, the more it is shared. The more it makes them like all the others who come here. They will learn that they are the only ones who called for their sacrifice. They will learn that they can swim very well in the waters that killed them. They will learn the difference between a bridge and a cave. They will learn that power, artfully applied, will disperse the stench of their baggage and dissolve its shackles. They will learn that beauty is born, is made, is fleeting and is forever. They will learn that transmutation comes from within and transmigration **is** grace. They will learn that **spectacle** and **sabotage** are the same thing. They will learn how to separate **water** (cleanse, pure, clear, deadly) from **fall** (dark, downward, separate, bury). They will learn that small threats breed and escalate and large threats transform and elevate. They will learn that memory lasts only as long as there is someone to remember, and someone will always be **here**. They will learn to tell black from white and which parts of them they match. They will learn to see gray for what it really is: a veil to *be penetrated, ripped away. They will learn that destruction is not the better part of valor, and what can and cannot be undone. Recon-structed. Erased. And the will learn that a waterfall is not a portal, it is only a waterfall.*

POST

She swims mythic waters
Bends their song
to her touch
Shared riverveins
spread her reflection
like waterfall mist

She is there

She is not there

She is there.

- C.

ABOUT THE AUTHOR

Kimberly White's poetry has appeared in *The Massachusetts Review, Cream City Review, Skidrow Penthouse,* and other journals and anthologies. She is the author of four chapbooks: *Penelope, A Reachable Tibet, The Daily Diaries of Death,* and *Letters to a Dead Man;* as well as two other novels: *Bandy's Restola,* and *Hotel Tarantula.* She also dabbles in collage art and photography, and spends most of her time in Northern California with her pens and papers and massive collection of Tarot decks.

WE PUT THE LIT IN LITERARY

clashbooks.com

FOLLOW US
TWITTER, IG, FB

@clashbooks